THE ARTONUEE HAD LONG KNOWN that their five worlds would eventually be destroyed. But the time was far, far away. And meanwhile, life was good.

The Mother was benign and wise. The ifflings thrived. Miaree—delicate, lovely Miaree—was on the verge of her joyous ripening and soon would choose a male to fertilise her eggs.

Meanwhile, there was the glorious blend of skill and ingenuity, the pure ecstasy of riding the gossamer-sailed drivers that flew between the Worlds, carried by the winds of space. Life was good indeed, and death, for the time being, only a completion, a new beginning.

There was nothing to fear . . .

THE LEGEND
OF MIAREE

Zach Hughes

BALLANTINE BOOKS • NEW YORK

SBN 345-23888-5-125

First Printing: April, 1974

Cover painting by Gene Szafran

Printed in the United States of America

BALLANTINE BOOKS
A division of Random House, Inc.
201 East 50th Street, New York, N.Y. 10022

1

You must understand, my children, that a fable is merely a fable. Understand, too, that although I am old, and reputed, by former students of certain perceptiveness, to know everything, there are things that even I do not understand. The best mind can be befuddled, for example, by the mere existence of the Q.S.S.'s beyond Cygnus, unbelievably far, unusually bright, deliciously mysterious.

We men are arrogant creatures. We measure and guess, within plus or minus a few light years, their distance, those objects which we cannot explain. We speculate endlessly. Ah, how we do speculate.

The fable. You have read your first assignment, of course. I think not even the most daring of you would face me had you not.

In reading the fable you must remember that the world, this world, that world, any world, was once young. Yes, even Trojan V, my young Alaxender. Once we crawled, we men, on the surface of the old earth, and even then we could look up and see the colliding galaxies in Cygnus.

Have you considered, Elizabeth, why man had to go to Cygnus?

Ah, primitivism, you say. The urge to hear and see the big bang. Yes, that is the nature of man. When star meets star—picture it, a giant and ancient blue star sending out a corona at fifty thousand degrees centi-

1

grade toward a cooler red star with a surface of only fifteen hundred degrees—man must be there to measure. We are the inchworms of the universe, glorying in our ability to be there, feeling superior as we observe the paroxysm of two island galaxies wheeling ponderously into the ultimate death dance.

Because of the myth of understanding, you say, Julius. Yes, you too, Leslie, know that myth. Know the parts to understand the whole. See stricken stars surge into death and know the secret of creation.

Has that theory worked in practice, my lovely Stella?

Are we more than we were, John of Selbelle III?

We live. I am proof of that. We spread the dubious vitality of mankind to the far ends of this galaxy. We have heard, not with our inferior ears, but with instruments, the scream of a planet seared in the rush of an expanding nova, and we have probed into the old star fields at the center to find—what? What, Elana?

The dead planets? Death?

Ah, how alone we are.

But the question was this—about Cygnus: Do we understand the whole more for having been to far Cygnus?

At first we tried to go back in time, to measure the prime big bang of creation. Unable to do so, unable to find help in our quest from races other than our own, we poured a portion of the wealth of an empire of worlds into a Cygnus expedition, and we found a burning world and this. This treasury of words. Oh, you may, at any time, by appointment (since it is a popular pastime and in great demand), see in the viewing rooms the ponderous dance of the dying galaxies, speeded into a motion which our frail life-span could not cover. This theory and that theory come forth and we know one more tiny part of our universe, but we are still unable to define it, no more than primitive man with his theory of the universe folding back upon itself.

Why do you shiver, Martha from Terra II? Why? Is

it the fear of an emptiness beyond the range of our strongest instruments?

We are mobile to an unbelievable degree. Parsecs are but moments to us in our known blink patterns. Yet the unknown exists, representing—what? Death? Fear? We whistle into the dark maw of creation and further our knowledge. For what? For pure knowledge? Ah, we have planets devoted to the worship of data. We usurp a world to store our facts. We have a planet with machines to work endlessly, simply to relate our vast store of words.

Our parent sun, my young Healer from the old world, is said to be billions of years old, and it is a Population I sun, a young star. There at the center, where the Dead Worlds mock us, the stars are ancient, but where there was once life there are only death and silence and a hell of radiation from the densely packed fields of stars, and in all the universe we are, father and son, my young Healer, still alone.

Forgive me, I ramble. The question of ultimate creation is not scheduled to be solved this early in the semester. Yes, you may laugh, Cecile. I congratulate you on being able to understand that I make a pleasantry.

We are here to discuss a fable, for so your learned men have labeled it, this story of Miaree, this slim volume, this handful of words. Consider it and what went into the making of it. It is the product of two civilizations. Made by one, salvaged from a charred world by another.

What does it mean? I will not have the arrogance to tell you that. It is for you to decide.

First, we must remember that the words are only our words, and thus, a feeble substitute for reality. The words are not necessarily those of Miaree, for we found the fable to be totally incapable of literal translation. There is, as a result, a certain lack of preciseness, and absence of definition. There are questions left unanswered. Was Rei a man, much like us, Alfred? Ah, you can't say? Don't be ashamed. Neither can I. Yet I can see him and I know him. He lives in my mind, and thus, although he is separated by an eon of time and by endless light years from our pleasant rooms, he exists, does he not?

When our race was young it looked up and saw the colliding galaxies. They will be colliding long after you and I, young friends, have joined Miaree in past time. And then, as now, there will be many questions and few answers; hopefully, men will still be trying to find answers, perhaps, as we do, through literature. For I consider literature to be a minute island of sanity in a sea of excesses of cold measurement and frantic amassing of data. We live, through literature, many lives. This is a blessing, I feel, comparable to those bestowed by our medical miracles, which give us the longevity to travel to Cygnus for the sole purpose of watching stars mash each other, and which allow us a surplus of years so that we may squander the youth of our children in studying a fable which gives no answers.

I was asked once, by a scientist, the purpose of my seat here. I confessed that I had no answer. I said that my work would not chart the voids beyond our deepest blink. I said that my teachings would not explain any reasons. The universe, I said, will continue to expand as I talk and after I cease to talk, and someday, if you are right, my scientist friend, it will slowly, over endless eons, slow, fail, and fall, to start the cycle again. Will you be there to measure that primeval rebirth? You say, I told him, that all matter began with hydrogen. If so, explain what happens when all the matter in the universe coagulates into one infinite mass and goes Boom!

In the face of such monumental questions, we are more concerned—are we not?—with today's lunch menu in the dining hall. Life is measured in microseconds in the day of the universe, and our sun is but a second in its life, my children. We must be content to live our lives on the rolling seas of the endless eons and to be thankful, as Miaree was thankful.

Thomax, would you please shake your friend La-Conius and remind him that sleeping is best done in barracks? Ah, thank you. Now, LaConius, since you exhibit such interest, perhaps you would condescend to open your volume to page 1 and begin to read, that we might savor the literary style of the translator computer so well developed by your fellows on Tigian.

2

In the beginning, God set the heavens aglow with a golden light to guide the feet of nocturnal travelers and to light the dense juplee forests so that hungry ifflings might continue their feasting on broad, fat leaves.

It was a blessing, the light, the broad splash of fire which appeared low in the evening sky and grew with the movement of The World to burn night away and to cover the dome of the sky with its glory.

From the lowly ifflings, God created Artonuee to love the beauty which fought the darkness. The light was good. And the Artonuee flourished and partook of God's wisdom and flew on the wings of the sun and, coming too near, angered Her.

For to gain a world, and another, Artonuee forsook God and, in punishment, were doomed.

She spake: From the ifflings you came. To the ifflings return, and in the end, to eternal fire.

And the fires in the darkness grew as the Artonuee grew, and their thunder could be heard, and the end was ordained not quickly, but with inevitable slowness—eternal death marching down the blackness, sending messengers of light and radiation to remind the Artonuee of their transgressions.

Struggling against God's anger, the Artonuee bellowed out into the cold void in drivers and sought refuge, but did not find it, being limited by God's divine will.

3

"Forgive me, Mother. I sin."

She bowed before the shrine of her dwelling, released her prayer. Around her, the soft silk of the walls glowed warmth and comfort, and through the spun covering of the viewer the fires of the night glowed the earth.

She had risen at a predawn hour in order to catch the shuttle driver.

Dressed for flight, her fragility cocooned in the protection of spacecloth, she pushed against the diaphragm of the entrance, felt it give, open, caress, close behind her. There in the night the sky was a sea of fires in blues and reds and yellows. She tuned her multifaceted eyes to drink the beauty and the awesome power of it, the variance of color and frequency, and the grim reminder, in halos of burning carbons and metals and gases, of the slow march of eternity. In her ears was the voice of God, on a non-utilitarian frequency, the scream of it, the roar of it; the tortured stars were knifing into her universe edge on, slightly inclined, wheeling star on star, worlds burning in terrible beauty.

She was young. As did all Artonuee, she reckoned her twenty years by The World out there up wind, where the ifflings crawled and fed on leaves. Maturing, she was considered beautiful. Life was sweet.

All senses open, she studied God's grandeur. The night sky reflects the power of God, and Her anger.

She looked on it as a child, wide-round eyes registering all, ears operative on all frequencies, and she was as a child, lying on a mossy hill behind her Chosen Mother's dwelling, hands under her head, looking up.

Individual, near stars were dimmed. The dome burned. And yet it was all so distant, the nearest flare magnified out of its importance by relative nearness. Small, insignificant stars streaming toward each other, blending, blossoming into space-eating hugeness. Flying downwind from such small stars would be, she knew, an exercise for a novice.

But to fly before the combined fury of their meeting?

She shivered. To be alive when the masses struck, to fly before the storm of winds *then*. On that wind she would fly forever into the impenetrable depths where life was too short. But to fly, once, on such force! To feel the beat of the wind on the wings of her flyer.

Such thoughts angered God. She pressed herself, indicating her defenseless heart to God. She felt deliciously sacreligious.

The words of the priests came back to her. "Space is God's dwelling," they said. Why, she asked, are males so much more devout than females? "You flaunt your sin before Her, flying. It is an arrogant repetition of the original sin, and it is useless. Have we not determined that we cannot flee Her? Forsake the ways of the wicked. Fight the whim in you, female, which calls you to defy Her."

"I die," she answered. "All Artonuee die. We see our doom in the night sky. Our world dies day by day. Our death comes toward us slowly, as stellar distances are measured, but inevitably. Our instruments can measure it. We ourselves can sense it. I, of course, will not be alive, in this body, at the end. That is Her will. But were I alive, I would watch the nearing of the colliding star through the thick viewer of my flyer. I would sail before it, the end, using its winds. I would watch the tendrils of the solar flames reach out, touch our worlds. And as I flew there, deep in space, all wings spread, catching the fury of the death of all, using it to reach a depth never before achieved by flyer, by Artonuee, I would ask Her: Why, Mother? No. I refuse to see that my flying makes the original sin—if, indeed, it were sin—any more reprehensible. Can we be punished more than once? We die. Meanwhile, I fly."

"God, in Her mercy, could decide to forgive," they said.

Males. Weak. Foolish. But then, they were changed without wings, never knowing the soar of it, the view of The World from aloft on the gentle winds of the air. "I read the Book," she told them. "It foretells all things and I find no promise of forgiveness. Can God, Herself, find a reversal for the inexorable movements of the universe?"

"Sacrilege," cried the male teachers, hiding their eyes from the possibility of God's immediate fury.

It was the nature of the female to think, to seek. During long hours under the night sky she watched the march of the galaxies and, in theory classes, talked of ways to beat God's laws. That she could not overcome the limitation of the speed of light saddened her, as it had saddened generations of Artonuee females. Yet, saddened, she still faced the impossible distance between the Artonuee galaxy and the nearest giant wheel which swam in clean space immune to the angry retribution of the Artonuee God.

Once, with her soul mate, she calculated the size of a driver large enough to carry juplee leaves for two ifflings and a host on a voyage through time to the far galaxy. Ifflings, given an unlimited supply of food, lived through the centuries. The host could be in dormant state.

The cubic area required for food alone dwarfed her imagination. Only the growing juplee forests could supply a greedy iffling with his food, and it was beyond Artonuee technology to transship a growing forest. Not even an imaginative Artonuee female could counter the immutable laws of a vengeful God.

You think thus, if you're an Artonuee female standing under the fires of the night. You shiver in your spacecloth and press your heart and force the sacrilege far down inside you and think, perhaps, of the long life which the race has already enjoyed and of how far it has flown from The World, green, cool, damp, how far from the ifflings the race has risen. Yet, one is not allowed to be prideful for more than a moment, for it is there, moving at thirty-five thousand miles per second, great sheets of stellar flame as stars embrace in paroxysmal finality. It is impossible to deny it. Not even if you are Miaree, aged twenty and feeling the first thrust of the formation of pre-eggs in your body. So you tuck your tiny, now useless wings close under the snug spacecloth, pick your way down the dew-dampened vault of the garden past the night-blooming flowers. You lean now and then, if you're Miaree and twenty, for there is no one out to see and laugh as you revert to childhood and, with your long, graceful, and marvelously flexible lips, drink nectar and laugh at yourself.

Up there the sun is beginning to light the tops of the low hills. The World wakens slowly. The first red rays reach and pierce and do battle with the cold light of the evil stars, and you tune out evil, using only part of your senses, and you run lightly to the roller where the meter shows more than enough charge to last the few moments of predawn required to drive the empty thoroughfare, wind moving the fine tendrils of your hair, dawning streets, an early riser keening a greeting, and in the burst of dawn the driver pointed upward, phallic, male, waiting and reaching.

4

Stinkpot driver pounding upward on primitive fire blackening the atmosphere. But even pollution can, at times, be beautiful, and the pull of the enforced gravity of the drive does not detract from the sheer joy of looking back to see the long trail as the driver gains cold air and speeds, screaming, into the dark side. Behind, as night moves in a knife-edge line, the distant stream of the contrail and the silk-puff clouds which are once individual and soft, looking as if one could walk, and then, from the heights, solid blankets, and then, higher still, overall whorls and patterns of the planet's weather. A huge circular movement on the southern seas, the shine of the ice cap of the north as the driver reaches height and apparent motion ceases, only the swimming of New World below giving an illusion of life in the stillness of near space.

The shuttle is not crowded. The days of leisure are ahead, but below the Artonuee labor industriously and only a few, on holiday, may seek the frivolity of work-period flying. To her left, a matronly woman, grown thick in age, soon to feel the debilitating call back home. In the seat to her rear a young girl, wearing the red-and-yellow badge of the learner, slightly nervous. First solitary flight, guesses Miaree, and feels a surge of empathy, a need to reach out and touch. Her mind seeks, is greeted. "Love, don't be afraid."

A burst of corrective fire, sending a tremble through

the driver, and the lingering, in the nostrils, of the smell of New World, gradually replaced, cycled out, as the air is reconditioned. And in the huge forward viewer, Flyer Haven. In the time it takes to reach it, drifting at mechanical speeds, she could have soared past Outworld. But there is patience mixed with her anticipation, for she has a long holiday. The *Rim Star* is provisioned and ready, according to her advance orders.

Flyer Haven gleams with inner light. The dome, slightly frosted by condensation from the interior, is a silver jewel in the black fur of the outer night. The main spread of the distant fires is hidden behind the planetary bulk, but shines out at the rims, haloing the globe, refracting blue on the fringes of the atmosphere. The good blue world, a paradise of hills and water and multicolored plant life, home, now. And out there, a half-inch circle of reflected light. The World.

A shuddering braking fire, then silence and a slightly discernable bump and the metallic sounds of the locks engaging, and she is standing, smiling encouragingly toward the novice, nodding with respect toward the graying veteran who amasses her carry baggage and nods in return, sending a pleasant "Good soar."

Ah, God, the wonderful smell of it. Flyer Haven. Enclosed, safe, old but constantly renewed. Flyer Haven, a senseless squandering of the wealth of the Artonuee, according to the reactionary males, who, from their minority seats in the Interplanetary Council, mount annual battles against it, for their natural caution and the slowness of their reactions bars them from partaking of what it offers. Flyer Haven, catharsis, reward, blood of life to those who have known the spread of thousands of yards of golden sail running before a sun storm.

Reused air, sweet, but marked by its mechanical treatment. A decorative and expensive touch there, at the inner lock, a planter of pleele, sweetest of the sweet, the look of which causes a stirring in the female breast and the breath of which, when pre-eggs are lodged and forming, is the most lovely of aphrodisiacs. She paused, closed her eyes in ecstasy, breathed long and deep. Then moving on the conveyor past the shops on the outer layer, the smell of a welder, acrid, cold, burning. The feel of a charge in the air as a convertor is tested, raising goose bumps on her, causing the fine, smooth fur of her body to ripple in sensation.

She stepped off the conveyor at Operations, left her carry baggage outside, stood before the officious male at the desk. "Miaree of the *Rim Star*. Ten days' provisions in place?"

"Ah." An incline of the head. Indifference. But, about her, a lingering aroma of pleele flowers. A widening of the eyes. "Miaree." The name is hissed.

It is, she suspects, closer than she thinks, although reading, she cannot tell. But this reaction from a young male tells her. She has seen it. And within her there is a fierce pride as she tilts her beautifully molded head imperiously and smiles. Poor male. When the time is near, he will be at his duty on Flyer Haven and she ...

On Outworld there are meadows nestled among the crags on which grow the Outworld wonders, the zoological garden of the Artonuee, a world given over to the fashioning of beautiful objects and to love ...

Close. She shakes her head. The heavy, flowing yellow of her hair moves, as if in slow motion, about her radiant face. Huge blue eyes blink, open to reflect, from their multifacets, the charge light of the arcs.

He is checking off the list. His male lips—why are they so suddenly of interest?—say the words. *Food. Necessities.*

"Ah, yes, ten days, Lady. Your credit voucher please?"

Even old Beafly notices. "The pleele flower is sweet," he says, as she stands next to him in his shop. He tinkers with a control circuit board from a Class II, a beginner's flyer with a feeble little convertor suitable only for orbital flights. "Yes, my daughter?"

"Indeed," she admits. "You finished the major on Rim Star?"

"Ah, a sweet ship." His hand trembles as he steadies a tool and jabs expertly into the innards of a complicated Mires expander. She, saddened, smells the age of him. "I have shared her secrets with young Runder."

"So soon, Beafly?" From her blue eyes the dew of the sadness she feels.

"It comes to all," he says, not looking at her. "Smelling the pleele as it clings to you, telltale, exciting, is my only reason for sadness."

"Perhaps ..." She pauses. It was Beafly who checked her out in her first Class II.

"No, daughter. See how the hand rebels?" He held it out in front of him. And she touched it. He smiled. "Could I but wait, I would break the rules and choose one of your ifflings, daughter."

"Thank you."

"A ten-day holiday?" He was at his work, not looking into her wide eyes. "Ten days. The signs are good. Weather predicts a flare."

"I know. I timed it so." She put her hand on his shoulder. "I am sorry, Beafly. Do you know when?"

"I want to walk, not crawl." He sighed. "Before you have flown and returned."

"Ah, no."

"I will like being there, once more. I find myself dreaming of the soft shade of the juplee. I hunger for the taste of the fruit and the coolness of its waters in my throat. Do you remember, daughter, how it tastes, the water?"

"Yes." Winglings hover and dive, splashing, thin membranes then weighted and grounded until the sun, stronger there on The World, dries them, and as they wait, the sweet fruit, snatched playfully from the powerful maw of a hapless iffling, the smell of the flowers, the taste of the water.

She had not kissed a male. "Beafly?" He turned, faced her. The thought caused her shapely backside to twitch, put life into muscles not yet used. He looked and smiled.

"Three times I have been chosen," he said. "Never did I see one so beautiful."

She leaned. Her long, flexible lips touched. He sighed and touched her; her thin waist felt the shaking of his old hands. And the agitated chemistry of her body flowed pleele flower aroma and filled the grimy workshop and left him dazed and weak as she broke the kiss.

"I would consider you," she said.

"I seek my ifflings happily," he said. His eyes were down.

"Perhaps I will see you in—someone—somewhere. I will know, should it happen."

"I pray so, daughter. May my iffling be kind. May I be wingling and like you, daughter."

Eyes turned as she passed, weeping. But one does not weep long on Haven. There is too much life. An exultant novice, being toasted at the head of a dock, having her hair sprinkled with wine. A grizzled veteran standing before a trim Class VI, spacecloth immaculate.

"Sister," Miaree greeted, pausing. "She is very lovely."

"She tends to yaw on a sunward track."

"But lovely. And such a flaw can be tuned out."

"My second Bertt," the veteran flyer said. "Good man, but I think influenced by the cold of Five. Too much weight in the insulation, I fear."

"My first was a Bertt," Miaree said. "A sweet Class II."

"And now?"

"A Corleu."

"Five?"

"Six."

"Ah. You have more hours than your youth would lead one to believe." There was a new respect in the older female's eyes. "I wanted a Corleu. The waiting list is unbelievable."

"I was lucky," Miaree said, putting one delicate foot on the outer rim of the Bertt VI, standing casually, spacecloth draping her form, eyes drinking it in, the long lines of sports flyers at the docks, the hustle and bustle of the Haven, the chargy smell of it, the feel of space outside pressing down, the nearness of the power of the sun, the feel of it through the dome warming her skin under her delicate fur.

"I wish more females would go into building," the veteran said. "There is a lightness. The feel of the wings, I suppose."

"Yes."

"Well, good flight."

Down the line a flyer warming, convertors charging at peak, rocking the ship at its moorings. The prickly feel of the charge restoring a full cheer to Miaree. And there, at the end of Dock Ten, *Rim Star*, the shape of the egg of an Artonuee female, graceful, shining outer hull decorated with the business instruments of flying, viewer large and all-encompassing, sail storage areas bulging like juplee fruit about to burst.

Inside, cushioned in the seat, checking the list. Nothing forgotten. She did not want to have to abort her ten-day flight. Not because some dock hand had made a bad count. Provisions, however, checked. "Operations, thank you. Check and receive."

"Acknowledged, *Rim Star*."

"*Rim Star* warming."

"Acknowledged and granted."

The purr of it, the great, sweet hum of it. Servos cutting in. Power crackling, making that delicious prickling feeling on her inner skin. Charges building. Weather on one frequency saying confirmation of the forecast with figures which sent a thrill of elation through her.

"Storm warnings for classes II through IV. Classes

II and III limited to local flying not exceeding ten minutes return."

Poor novice. The one on the shuttle.

"Class V warning. Winds may exceed structural design limitations in the vicinity of One Planet."

"*Rim Star* warmed. Charge check. Convertors check. Sails check. Navigation request, unlimited. Request clearance and lift."

"Acknowledged and granted, *Rim Star*."

Ahead of her the Bertt VI, lifted on the arms of the giant crane, cradled tenderly in padded holds.

"Stand by, *Rim Star*."

Dock boys appearing, chattering, running, laughing. Lucky lads. Sacrificing immortal souls to work on the fringes of wonder, to see the flyers being lifted, to hear the hum of convertors. The muted contact of the lift arms, movement. Above, the lock. Front view. Frosted dome. A push and contact with the lock and an end to the artificial gravity of Haven. A lifting in her seat against the belts, the freedom of space. A surge of elation and the hiss of evacuating air and then the instruments registering the cold of naked space on the hull and the convertors humming. The outer door opening and out there down the tunnel of the lock the cold stars, the lock faced away from New World.

"Guidance jets ready," she sent.

"Cleared."

"Charging."

"Acknowledged."

"Mass unit one-minus and lowering." The meters spinning, measuring mass of the flyer, minutely calibrated, dials glowing, hands making swift revolutions and her wide eyes following. "God, they're cooking today." The exclamation thoughtless. No place for personal observations and chat-chat on the control channels. "Sorry, control."

"Convertor efficiency?" asked the cold, male voice of control.

"Eighty-five-point-nine and lowering."

"Cleared."

"Ninety and lowering."

"Good flight, *Rim Star*."

"Ninety-eight-point-nine, steady. Expel, please."

"Acknowledged."

A movement. There is a strange feel about a flyer at charge. Skin tingles. Hair seemed to be individually electric. Fur is alive. With satisfaction she noted the excellence of old Beafly's tune-up. Mass lowered, as the flyer moved along the tube and leaped. Never had she seen the convertors working so efficiently. The mass of her flyer, and herself, and all the provisions and the bottle of jenk liquor in her carry baggage, all lowered, lowered to within a few points of nonexistence. The miracle of Lonwee the Ancient, the conversion of mass, the Lonwee principle which made flying possible.

"*Rim Star* clear. Sails."

Click. Servos moving in near silence, sensed by feel. The gravitational field of New World the controlling factor as she unfurled billowing yards of diaphanous sails, extending the area of space commanded by *Rim Star* tenfold, a hundredfold, and more. The weak force of New World's gravity now negated as the winds of the sun blew, and off on a wing, sails tilted, Haven diminishing in an instant. Massive acceleration as the quiet wind moved.

She entered a new world. A world of quiet and peace. One last word. "Haven, *Rim Star*. Systems check. Exit path 180 reverse from Haven. Sunward inclination 45. *Rim Star* out, requesting privacy. Emergency frequency seven on monitor."

"*Rim Star*, good flight."

The World was in opposition, on the away side of the sun. First Planet was oblique on its near orbit, a growing dot as wind speeds were achieved, the flyer drifting across the wind on a tight tack, orbit spiraling, decreasing. *Rim Star* was a mote in space, near weightlessness, near zero inertia. Huge sails were battered by the force of the eternal wind, the flow of particles from the furnace which grew and gained a corona visible to the naked eye. And it was her world, her life. Below, she was valuable, a worker. Here she was Miaree of the Artonuee, female, free, flying. Here there was a play for all her senses, measuring, sensing, feeling, tasting, calculating. Fingers flew at the console keys, asking the lightning synapses of the mechanics to aid her own senses, for at wind speeds the brain was a poor, slow thing. And the distances, interplanetary, which once had cost lives and the wealth of The World, which were fearful chasms for the primitive drivers, were but winged thoughts for a mote flying at wind velocity, even beating sunward as the computer lowered mass reduction to use the gravity of the sun itself to hasten the fall toward the burning light.

First Planet grew. Barren. Magnified by the scope of the viewer, it glared reflected light and spun its flattened hills there so near the furnace that no life grew and surface temperatures reached fearful intensity on sunside.

The chronometer clicked. But it alone measured time. For Miaree, time was back there, on New World and Haven. When she was hungry, she ate. When she was thirsty, she drank. The flyer was cramped, but she was at home in it. As she established a spiral approach and locked in, she sang. The tune was old, old as The World, a melody keened by winglings learning. And as her heart soared, she slipped the spacecloth and was herself, slim, delicately formed, shapely. She stretched her long legs and, in unashamed narcissism, admired them, the knees, perfect. The long muscles slim and graceful. Slim waist. Lovely torso. Long neck. And all of it furred sweetly, delicately, electric to the touch as her hands smoothed it from its long captivity in the spacecloth.

Naked Miaree, freed in space in the wings of *Rim Star*. Keening melody from her throat. Reaching for the jenk liquor and sipping, for she needed no further intoxication toward happiness. Happiness was flying out there close to God, and if God, being a selfish wench, abhorred company and doomed a race for Her privacy, a pox on her.

For she was Artonuee and female and daring and was not to be held to the ground. Had not God Herself instilled the love of flight? God wanted Artonuee to fly, so She gave them wings and then, in a fit of rancor, took them, leaving only the memory; and when males said the driver was ultimate and took the race from The World to New World, Outworld, and Five, the great Lonwee said nay, and made the first convertor and flew alone and gave back the gift taken by God in spite.

She was Artonuee and doomed, but she flew, and the sun gave her energy and the sails used it and the convertors hummed and gravity was the rudder, and down, down, down she soared on the wings of the solar wind, until with First Planet on the sunward wing, sails baffling on a hard tack, she was near, near to the source, the heat of it, the power of it.

And to the appointed minute, the storm rose out of the white fury of the sun, an enormous flare, a hurricane of energy. Vast thermonuclear fusion reactions gutted a portion of the sun's disc, and she felt it, felt her naked fur stand and quiver, and sails set, she waited as the winds came blasting up at thirty-seven thousand miles per second, and mass reduced to the limit of the straining convertors, the *Rim Star* leaped before the storm, a mote in darkness, and fled down the wind, leaving First World in the distance and passing the orbit of The World as Miaree sang the song of flight and felt the sails strain under the onslaught.

She drank jenk as she flew past New World, letting the sweet bite of it add to her exhilaration, a tipsy, slim, beautiful Artonuee female in flight, soaring on the light of the sun, riding the most wonderful storm she'd ever had the fortune to meet. Singing, feeling the pre-eggs in her lower abdomen, letting the jenk liquor surge through her bloodstream, disobeying the rules of flight but high, high, loving it, singing it, lithe and naked in the padded chair, watching the flow of particles with a part of her senses and seeing New World pass swiftly and looking off on a tangent to sight Outworld and, thrilled, remembering the sweetness of it on the viewers and knowing that she'd be there soon, not merely passing it on the fury of a solar storm, but there, on its surface.

Three days later, when the wind speed had dropped to a mere one million miles per hour, lonely in the outback, past the orbit of Outworld and nearing the area of Five, where the strange male builder, Bertt, chose to set up his flyer works in the eternal cold, she was feeding on concentrated juplee fruit and feeling mournful, for soon the wild ride would cease to be free and easy, and the major portion of her holiday would be spent in beating back, laboriously and with a tedious slowness, toward New World and Haven. Yet that in itself was pleasure, the ultimate challenge. Only a Class VI could do it. Only a Corleu VI, female built, could do it in the time allotted to her.

Now there was time, full time, boring time, time to be devoted to study of her techniques and time to merely sit, viewer on full magnification, and look at the lights of God, for out here they seemed so near. Like a broad band of arcs, they covered the viewer, sharp outlines undistorted by atmosphere. And she could see the titanic joining of two globular clusters on the angle of the far rim, thick with stars in collision, the single loudest object in the near sky.

She herself, in *Rim Star*, had moved faster than the stars.

There were times, in contemplation, when she fought against the traditional sense of doom. Galactic distances are not compatible with the life-span of even an Artonuee female, and it was, in a sense, strange to know the racial feeling of impending death when generation upon generation would crawl and fly and walk and return and there would be no apparent change in the fires of the night. It was all relative, and the approach of death for the race, at thirty-five thousand miles per second, was a chilling concept unless one related it to time, and then, if one were irresponsible—and, at times, during flight, the female can be irresponsible, witness her flouting of the ironclad rule against intoxicating liquids aboard a flyer—it could be ignored.

True, determine the ages before the good sun burned and fused, and it seemed futile to carry the load of doom on shapely, winged shoulders. And yet, nagging at her was that racial consciousness, that something, that link.

All Artonuee being one, riding the single life-force allotted to them—and, perhaps, to the entire galaxy, since all attempts at communication with intelligent races theorized to inhabit other systems had failed—there was the heaviness of knowledge that the beauty would die, that life would cease and be replaced by the fires of God in cold space.

Thus, with a mercurial change of mood, she saddened and remembered the old mech at Haven, bless him. Old Beafly and his appointment on The World. It came to all. It would come to her and that part of her which was aware would sink, be replaced with another awareness, and although there was a link, a feeling of oneness, Miaree as Miaree would cease to be.

But not now. Not with the wings atilt and beating up the wind slowly, gaining speed as the computer advanced mass just enough to seize the sun's far pull and use it. Not with the planets wheeling in the viewer. Not with the pre-eggs making themselves felt and the lingering scent of pleele in her, somewhere. Now she lived and flew, and *Rim Star* strained and creaked its hull as opposing forces buffeted it, and she was near Outworld, homebound, able to see the Outworld shuttle belch upward on an arc of fire and to see Outgate swimming in space, destination of lovers.

In the storm, the interplanetary magnetic fields were strengthened, and reading them, she knew once again the love of her system, knew the prickling of its forces, and it was impossible to be melancholy.

She sang.

A song of love, of dreams, of endless bliss.

Between the orbits of Outworld and home, she flitted among moon-sized planetoids, playing with disaster casually, displaying a navigational skill attained by few flyers as, just for the pure hell of it, she did a complete orbit of a jagged, spinning, juggernaut of death in the form of a rock which would have filled the inland sea of The World. *Rim Star* could do it. She could do it. So that made it necessary for them to do it and laugh, the slow wheeling of the jagged rock portside, near, so near she could see, slightly magnified, that diamonds studded the barren rock. She noted and ran the orbit of the rock into her on-board course recorder. It would be duly reported and, perhaps, if the find was important enough, would add to her flight time in the form of a reward for exploitable discovery. It was highly unusual, the find. And it was sheer accident, happy accident. The asteroid belt had been picked clean, said the veterans, who spent much time there in the early days of flight.

And that made the long flight something to be remembered. She would not let her high hopes build to a level of potential disappointment, but there was the possibility. It was a small rock, and that, perhaps, explained its being unknown, uncharted. And yet there was a possibility that some flyer in centuries past had found it, reported it, and had been disappointed to find, after exploration by a mining driver, that it was not worthy of exploitation.

She luffed, drew closer. Fist-sized stones, gleaming and, to her eyes, perfect, shone in the viewer at full magnification. She rechecked the in-flight recorder, making sure that the coordinates recorded there would lead a mining driver to the rock.

She had lost speed. To regain it, it was necessary to orbit with the belt, mass equalized with pull. And a new course had to be plotted. Busy with it, she started when, with a piping complaint, the sensors told of another flyer, approaching from outward. She noted its distance, continued with her calculations. Finished, she addressed herself to the intruder.

Amazingly, it was approaching on a direct line, heading toward the asteroid belt at storm speed. No, faster. Unbelievingly, she watched as her instruments confirmed the speed and bulk. No flyer, that. Not driving directly into the wind. And a driver coming head on at the belt? Were they mad?

"Danger, danger," she sent, on all frequencies, emergency and communicative. "To unknown driver in Area Y-23-5-A, you are on collision course with belt. Veer off."

She listened. From Outworld she heard communicators. A mining driver in the belt identified itself. There was no communication from the driver, which, at strange speeds, came toward her.

She turned communicators to maximum peak, repeated her warning. And now the viewer picked up the approaching driver and measured it. Mass, size. Incredible. Her heart leaped. God!

In all of the system there was no driver of that size. In all of the system no driver of that configuration.

She flashed the system-wide danger signal in all forms, visual, auditory. Light flared from the nose of the driver, and it was braking, but too late. It swept into the belt at a speed which she had not matched at the height of the storm's fury, going outward. With its speed and mass, it weaved only slightly, picking its way. It passed within thirty thousand miles of her, and at first she hoped that due to its incredible maneuverability, it would pass through untouched. The brief bursts of light, comparable to the light of flares on the sun, seemed to be immensely powerful. The driver was using the force of the sun and that made it absolutely certain that it was not of the Artonuee system. And there was a feeling of awe about her, watching, praying. Behind, the blackness of space was fired by the massed, exploding stars and there, in local blackness, the fires of a miniature sun as the alien blasted a terrible curve past still another hard, faceted chunk of rock; she could not believe that anything could withstand the stresses of that curve. And then it was making it, followed by her instruments, a blip now on the full screen of the viewer, but almost past, free, almost, in the emptiness of interplanetary space toward New World, a shower of tiny particles, a wall of inertial force as tangents merged and the alien struck, small asteroids bouncing away, larger ones doing terrible damage, and with a crunching finality, the almost head-on contact, at that awesome speed, with the parent rock of the cluster. The alien spun, wheeled ponderously, regained straight-line flight, but it was visibly limping, losing air into all-devouring space as Miaree accelerated, tacking toward it. Her speed matching the speed of the alien now, then overtaking.

Something had spewed into space. Her sensors warned, and she avoided the trail of entrails. Maximum magnification showed the objects to be inanimate, some mechanical, parts ripped and torn from the skin of the alien driver.

With a start, she saw the front of the driver light, braking again. Now it was in the pull of the sun and its original speed was a terrible handicap. The lights of the braking were seemingly weaker. Again and again they flashed, as if in desperation. Still the sunward momentum was in command.

And there was nothing she could do. Even an Artonuee driver could not outdistance a flyer on a sunward track. And as the alien driver accelerated, she saw it pull away.

God, it was unfair. All the years of speculation, of hope, of effort. All the wealth poured into sending unreturned signals into space. And there it was, a driver, a driver from out, and it was diving for the sun on a straight line and would plunge into the furnace in—she calculated—three days.

It was unfair to her and to all Artonuee and it was unfair to the beings on board the doomed flyer. For there, in that battered hulk, was the secret to resist God. To come to the Artonuee system, the driver had had to cross interstellar space. And, unless it was an incredibly old robot machine, it had had to fly at a speed which proved, with finality, that God's laws were not absolute.

These were her thoughts as she chased futilely after the runaway miracle from the stars. And as it passed the orbit of New World, no longer blinking in that desperate effort to break its fall into the sun, she felt a surge of despair.

Lost. Irretrievably lost. Salvation for the race within her sight and now gone. A blip on the viewer, a tiny particle lost in the vastness of space. Accelerating with the sun's pull. Leaving her behind as she forgot her flight plan and went past New World in the desperate hope that, at the last minute, a miracle would happen.

She lost the driver in the fires of the sun as it passed the orbit of First Planet, and far from home, overdue, she once again rode the winds outward, but no longer ebullient. Saddened. Shamed at her inability to help.

They were broadcasting her call when she opened the communicators. She edged into Haven, a half-day overdue. The committee awaited at the dock. A stern male boarded *Rim Star* and confiscated the in-flight recorder.

She was numbed, helpless. It was only when the controller picked up the empty bottle, the jenk liquor bottle, that she was able to submerge her sadness in common sense. The flight recorder would contain her frantic messages to the alien, the messages which had been, apparently, unheard. And such things were not for mere males. There was meaning here. Males, hearing her description of the alien, would say, "It is only the jenk."

"I plead immunity on the grounds of discovery," she said, as the stern-faced male looked at her.

"That is a serious statement. Don't make it worse, my daughter, by clutching at motes in the wind."

"Nevertheless, I plead," she said. "And I request direct transport to Nirrar to report my discovery." There was the diamond asteroid, of course, but it was not that now diminished discovery which concerned her. She wanted to talk with Mother Aglee. The asteroid would cover her movements.

"And this?" The controller was holding the empty bottle. "Does pleading discovery excuse this flagrant breach of regulations?"

"I will face that," she said. "I will accept my penalty."

"It is usual to withdraw flying rights."

"For how long?" Her heart was hurting. Not to fly?

"A year. More."

Oh, no, she thought. Oh, no.

"We will put a seal on the flyer," the controller said, "until the hearing."

5

The small executive driver which lowered her to the Nirrar port was luxurious and comfortable, but the pleasure was lost on her. In her mind, she could hear the disintegrating whine of metals, the crackle of liquid fire, could imagine the terminal pain of burning. She could see, with her large eyes lidded, the strangely fashioned driver as it plunged sunward. She closed off all sensation, became encased in her body, suffered with the beings aboard the driver, dead by now.

She lifted her privacy screen only when the crush of deceleration weighted her body. She was alone in the passenger section, was standing when the flight crew sent clearance and the outer door hissed, then lowered. Laden with carry luggage, still dressed in spacecloth, she walked from the pad, registered incoming, saw the fare charged to her personal credit. In the warm sun of New World, she stood, hair mussed, smelling chargy from ten days of flying, waved to a public roller.

She knew the city well. They gave the driver directions, waved aside his objections. "It's shorter to take the river road, lady," he said.

"And fight bumper to bumper traffic as the home-bound government employees are released," she said. "The Western Circle, then Lonwee Avenue."

"It's your credit, Lady."

Her own dwelling was on the outskirts to the north, in the residential complex around Research Quad. Just off the Western Circle, the new route finished only years in the past, was the home of her Chosen Mother, where she had learned and where she had grown. There were the schools, the parks, the playgrounds.

Near the port, the industrial complexes towered cleanly over the even elevation of the Nirrar Plateau, a site chosen for the capital city of the Northern Continent, a site picked after two centuries of unplanned city development proved to be disastrous for the newly settled planet. Nirrar was new, and yet it was old. In the Nirrar Hall of Wonders she had stood, with youthful awe, before the ancient and battered driver which, two thousand years ago, had first orbited New World. The Hall, itself, was of neo-silk construction and bore a date, over its ornate entrance panel, which established it as one of the first constructions of New Nirrar, following the first two centuries of planetary exploitation which had almost devoided New World of its native flora and fauna.

She loved the city, had roamed its avenues and byways, knew the secrets of its hidden, small dining halls, its tiny, out of the way shops where the exotic products of the five-planet system were on display. She had taken University at The School of the Artonuee, New World, in Nirrar Gardens, to the south of the main complex. Between her fourteenth and fifteenth years, she had served her mandatory aideship in the Hall of Government, starting as a mere clerk and, in one short year, had established a rank which had, to a young girl just out of University, seemed exalted. As assistant to the Charge Advisor in the government of Mother Aglee, she had appeared before the Planetary Legislature to testify on the negative results of the work of government scientists. She had been complimented by Mother Aglee herself on the clarity of her report on the ill-fated expedition to the sunside of First Planet. At the end of her year, she was offered permanent tenure and stood in line to be Charge Advisor when Lady Jonea, who was aging, should hear the call home. Her rank, when she reluctantly refused the permanent appointment, opting to pursue her chosen career in research, was awarded on a non-pension basis, but that rank, she knew, would assure her an audience with the Mother.

"Lady," the roller driver said, as he cruised Lonwee Avenue in ideal conditions, "I bow to you."

She accepted the compliment. He had the accent of the cold outworld, Five. "Just in?" she asked.

"A year, just shy," he said. "It would have taken a half-hour longer my way."

Since no vehicles were allowed in the Government Quad, she stepped out of the roller at the Southern Gate, had her credit stamped, joined a throng of sightseers on the public conveyors as they moved into the building complex past the impressive neo-silk and metal mounments to past Artonuee heroines. She soon branched into lesser-used paths, entering, at last, an executive conveyor, after showing her pass of permanent rank, and was whisked into the heart of the Quad. The Palace of the Mother towered over all in shining beauty, tall, many-viewered, guarded more out of ancient ceremony than of necessity, by the brightly uniformed Home Squad, tall, young men of seemingly equal attractiveness.

"I am Miaree, Rank Three, former assistant to Charge Advisor Jonea. I would see the Mother." She stood at respectful attention before the appointment clerk, which in itself was not a small feat, having required an hour of rank-pulling and demands.

"Your purpose?" asked the clerk.

"A matter of security," said Miaree. "Pass my name. Tell the Mother that I, Miaree, assure her of the urgency of my business. This I pledge."

The clerk looked at papers. "Could it have to do with a charge of intoxication while flying?"

Miaree's eyes changed from blue to an imperial purple, flashing anger. "Don't talk like a male fool."

To the female clerk, it was the ultimate insult. Her

honey-colored neck fur undulated as she swallowed her furious reply, for the rude female was Rank Three, permanent.

"I will not accept the responsibility," the clerk said, her thoughts colored with fire.

"Will you pass the responsibility, then?" Her tone told the clerk she had best do it.

"Wait, Lady." The title was delivered in a surge of sarcasm. The clerk disappeared into her inner office. Miaree put her carry baggage on the floor and waited impatiently. "Lady Jonea will see you," the clerk said, after an interminable period of time.

"I know the way," Miaree said, picking up her carry luggage and walking, back straight, rear tucked arrogantly, past the clerk's desk into the great hall.

Lady Jonea rose, extended both arms, embraced her. "Ah, the chargi19ness of you," she said.

"I came in great haste, Lady," Miaree said. "Forgive my spacecloth."

"The smell of you takes me back to my youth," Jonea said. She was gray. The look of her shocked Miaree. She had a flash of old Beafly. Now he was carrion on The World. "You come directly from flying?"

"Yes, Lady. I—"

"Good soar? Tell me." Jonea had embraced her, released her, regained her seat behind the huge desk with a sigh of weariness. "I have not flown . . ." She let her eyes lid, dreaming of it.

"Lady, I must see the Mother on a matter of utmost urgency."

"She will see you, of course."

"It grieves me to rush," Miaree said.

"I understand." The instrument on her desk was a direct link. It accomplished the results within seconds.

"Come with me," Miaree requested, "for the information I have is directly related to your work. Our work." And there were three of them in the surprisingly small office when Miaree began her report by playing back the in-flight recordings of her warning message to the driver pounding into the belt.

Lady Jonea was stiffly upright in her chair. Mother Aglee, younger than Jonea, but showing tired lines around her mobile lips, rested her chin in her hand.

Miaree waited comment. There was none. Jonea looked at her, face drawn in thought. "Ladies," Miaree said, "it was not an Artonuee driver."

"No," Mother Aglee said simply.

"I beg your pardon?" Miaree asked, surprised by the lack of reaction.

"A tragedy," Mother Aglee said, shaking her handsome head. "A tragedy."

"Mother, please, do you understand?" Miaree was leaning forward in her intensity. "It was not an Artonuee driver. It used as power a source which gave the same radiations as the sun, though not so intense, of course."

Mother Aglee rose, ran a delicate hand down the front of her robe of state. She opened a drawer, withdrew a carefully protected packet, motioned toward Miaree. Miaree rose, accepted the packet, looked at Mother Aglee questioningly. "Open it," Mother Aglee said.

The pictures were on duppaper, slick, indistinct in image. "We received these three years ago," Lady Jonea said. "There are many more. These were the first and came from a great distance."

The pictures were simple drawings, reproduced in dots on the duppaper. There were scars and slashes of static, but the images were discernible. A planet circled a sun, a rim sun, position indicated by a superimposed drawing of the galactic wheel. Picture two was three figures. Biped. Different, yet near the Artonuee form. A larger figure, naked, male genitalia evident. A medium-sized figure, the male identification absent. A small figure with smaller male genitalia.

Stunned, Miaree looked up. Mother Aglee smiled encouragingly. "Life," she said. "Intelligent life."

Miaree turned the next image. Stylized stars in collision, an arrow locating the planet. So near. Strange figures along the arrow.

"We think the figure represents God's Constant," Lady Jonea said. "We have been working on it. Note that there are stylized rays alongside the figure."

"Yes," Miaree breathed. "It would be less than one unit, but are their units the same?"

"God's Constant would be measured, in all probability, in relation to the planetary year. We would have to know—"

"The constellation of Delan!" Miaree said. "Figure of the mythical beast."

"Yes."

"But we have not been able to see it since—"

"Since the collision in Delan," Lady Jonea said. "Over two thousand years ago."

"Then they are dead," Miaree said.

"The last image," Mother Aglee said.

From the planet, a blunt arrow. Behind the arrow, a glare of light. A driver. Beside it more figures.

"As nearly as we can guess," Lady Jonea said, "this figure represents a multiple of God's Constant."

"Yes," Miaree said. "It would have to be. But—"

"Two years ago we started receiving these," Mother Aglee said, thrusting another packet onto Miaree. Miaree opened, looked.

"A course in language?" Miaree asked.

"For children," Lady Jonea said. "Basic numerology. The next one advances to the periodic table, a universal language."

"I don't understand," Miaree said. "No one knew. I mean, there was no word."

"We thought it best," Mother Aglee said.

"But everyone could hear. These are strong."

"How often do you monitor the electromagnetic bands above thirty thousand megacycles?"

"Not since University," Miaree admitted. "Not since we studied the attempts at interstellar communications." She fidgeted. "But I still don't understand. Why would you keep such a great event a secret?"

"Look at the first picture," Mother Aglee said. "The first one in the second packet."

It was past the language lessons. There was, once again, that obviously male figure, hand extended. On one side of the figure was the planet in Delan. On the other, an unmistakable representation of the Artonuee system. Miaree recognized the drawing of her system. It was a copy of the elementary messages sent during the abortive attempt at interstellar communications.

"It is a friendly gesture," she said, indicating the man's outstretched hand.

"Perhaps," Mother Aglee admitted. "Other observations?"

"An opportunity to learn their secrets. The power of the sun in some sort of driver engine. Speeds which would free us—"

"More basic observations, please," Mother Aglee said.

"I don't understand."

"He is quite obviously male," Lady Jonea said.

"I see," Miaree said, nodding. "And in the group picture, he is represented first. A male-dominated society?"

"With the scientific knowledge to negate God's Constant," Mother Aglee said. "And you yourself made an astute observation when you first looked at the selection of messages which were obviously sent from a driver in flight between stars. You said, as I recall, that it was a language for children."

"No," Miaree said. "It was Lady Jonea who said it was a lesson for children. I merely looked on it as being basic."

"Nevertheless," said Mother Aglee, "we must, in contacting such a race, behave with extreme caution. Observe the configuration of the alien male. Long, powerful arms, rounded. Like our males and yet unlike them, more powerful by far, it would seem. We must consider this apparent advantage. As we must consider others. Obviously, their technology is advanced. If they can best God's Constant, what else can they do?"

"Perhaps," Miaree said, "they have not been shackled in their research by hysterical males who scream sacrilege each time someone suggests that a new idea is not a repetition of the cardinal sin."

"Be that as it may," Mother Aglee said, "we are faced with a problem."

"It would seem to me, Mother, that our problem now is reduced to floating atomic particles on the surface of the sun," Miaree said.

"It is?" The older female sighed. "The planet of the aliens, in Delan, is very near the impact point of the stars. I feel that an advanced society, capable of star flight, will not be content with sending one driver to dive into the sun. That we must accept as very possible fact. I feel, daughters, that we will yet have our opportunity to meet these males from Delan face to face. We must be prepared. It is fortunate that it was you, Miaree, who saw the alien driver, for I have been considering, with much mental anguish, the necessity of sharing our secret with someone, someone capable of taking the alien messages and absorbing this language lesson for children. It was to be someone in the Research Quad, of course, but until today, I must confess that you had not occurred to me. Since you know, and are qualified, the choice is now made."

"There is one possible complication, Mother," Miaree said.

"Yes," Mother Aglee said, "under the aroma of charge I did detect it. Congratulations, daughter. Your ifflings will be a welcome addition to the stores of Artonuee life. I think, however, that you will find time for both."

"I will try," Miaree said, bowing her head.

6

Thank you, LaConius, you read well, even if your Tigian accent is a bit much at times. You must work on that, you know. Provincialism is the bane of our growing family of worlds. Unarrested, it could lead to dire results. Examples of provincialism, Alaxender?

Sir, the War of Zede II would be an example.

A good one. Thank you, Alaxender. Provincialism leads to nationalism. On the isolated planet of Zede II it was allowed to grow. Until, as one would cut out a cancerous growth, we eliminated it. But we are diverted. Impressions and summation, if you please, in the time remaining to us today. Cecile?

I like her. I like her very much.

Not the most astute of comments, Cecile. Why do you like her?

I don't know, really. She's young and beautiful and intelligent. Everything a woman should be.

But is she a woman?

Obviously. Different, but still beautiful.

Describe Miaree. Julius?

I donno—

Don't know.

I don't know, sir. I see sort of a—well, she's sorta weird.

Sort of. Yes, Stella.

Not weird at all. Not like us, naturally, having evolved on a totally different planet, under totally dif-

36

ferent evolutionary conditions. I see her as being light and almost elfin.

The term elfin is not definite, but is merely a word out of mythology. Continue, Stella.

Well, sir, she's almost birdlike.

No.

Yes, LaConius?

Sir, like a Tigian butterfly.

Ah!

Even to the life cycle. She has wings. And the— what are they? The winglings. They fly. And I see the ifflings as caterpillars, crawling around the woods eating leaves.

Yes, but if you had finished your assignment, La-Conius, you would have seen, although there is a certain correlativity, that ifflings are not caterpillars.

Well, sir, maybe not in the same shape. But the cycle is the same. Butterflies begin as eggs and then go through the larval stage, then into chrysalis, and finally emerge as winged creatures, fully adult.

But the writer speaks of a third change in the Artonuee.

Sir.

Elizabeth.

Since the Artonuee are much more complicated beings, perhaps the third change is necessary. In fact, in chapter—

Good, Elizabeth. Since you have obviously read ahead, describe Miaree.

I agree with LaConius, that she is like a butterfly. She has a sort of light fur. It could be like the minute scales on a butterfly. It's soft and not at all unbeautiful. And she has those long lips. She drank from a flower. Yet it was a thing she did only under cover of darkness and in privacy, indicating to me that it is only the young of the species, the winglings, who live on flower nectar. I think Miaree must be biped, for she is so described. And she apparently has only two arms. There is a hint toward her general shape in the mention of her—ah—rear. Apparently, the rear is, perhaps, more developed than in our races. And apparently, sexual connotations were present, since Miaree is aware of something, the eggs in her.

Very good. Any additions?

She has beautiful eyes, quite like the eyes of an insect, I think, large and blue and pretty.

Yes, Leslie. John?

We have butterflies on Selbelle III. I think they were imported from LaConius' home world, because our native life forms are rather like lizards. I thought of them when I drew Miaree. Would you like to see?

With pleasure.

Ah, you will be an artist, John?

Sir, I am an artist. I am from Selbelle III.

My mistake, sir. Yes, I agree. Class?

I think the head should be larger.

The rear should be more pronounced, like the body of a butterfly.

She should have a large head. And I think she should be slimmer, more graceful.

I think John has done a wonderful job with her. She's just as I see her. I could love her, I think.

Ah, Alfred, I see that you, too, have completed the assignment. Already thinking ahead? Romantically inclined. We have not heard from Clear Thought.

Sir, one thing we've not mentioned. She has at least rudimentarily developed telepathic abilities. She sent a message, while on the shuttle driver, to a novice flyer.

Good point, my young Healer.

Sir, I think her voice would be of great interest. The word keening is used at least once. As a musician, I think she would sing her speech much like the birds of the old worlds. A musical, high tone. Perhaps, as Clear Thought suggests, partially mixed with telepathy.

Very good, Elana. Now, from Miaree let us turn to the Artonuee society. Tomax?

A matriarchy, sir. With no real equality between the sexes. The males, I gather, are lesser creatures, unable to do some of the skilled things done by the females. The males are slower of reflex and exhibit some of the weaknesses usually associated with women.

Weaknesses? Ha!

Please don't interrupt, Cecile. Go on, Tomax.

The males are involved in the religion to a greater extent than the females; in fact, they seem to have put brakes on the development of Artonuee technology by imposing a set of taboos. I get the impression that since the Artonuee are acutely aware of a very slow process of destruction of their galaxy, they are an old race. We know, for example, that the city of Nirrar is almost two thousand years old, and the Artonuee went out to the planets from their home world at least two thousand years before the time of the story. So, their technology, although spectacular in some areas—notably the development of the convertors which reduce the mass and inertial forces of the flyers—must have developed slowly. I would guess that the beauty-loving females, although curious, showed little interest in technology prior to the invention of the flyer. The slow and dependable drivers are, I'd think, the products of the male mind. Yet, the males, in the hold of their superstitions, refuse to think in terms of overcoming the limitation of the speed of light, or, as they call it, God's Constant. There is evidence, in the reading so far, that the females, somewhat less inhibited by the burden of their God, are thinking in terms of advancements; but they, too, being products of their own civilization with its built-in limitations, find it difficult to accept, even in their irreverence, the possibility of God's being proven wrong in something so basic as the Constant. I think they're in for one hell of a cultural shock when the word gets out beyond government circles that someone, the men from Delan, has bested God's Constant.

Anything to add to that, Alaxender?

The females seem to be happy, sir, in their little flyers, loafing around the system like Sunday sailors on a lake. In a very feminine way, I think, they actually rather enjoy the drama of being doomed and aren't too eager to change the status quo.

Yes, Elizabeth.

I don't want to make this a battle of the sexes, but it is the females who are advancing the civilization. Not the males. They, pardon the expression, man the Research Quad and the government and they have the sense of adventure. The males plod and pray.

Who do you think wrote about Miaree? Yes, Martha.

A female, obviously. Otherwise, the flying segment could not have been so vividly described. A male who had never flown in a flyer could not have done it.

And the purpose of the book? Leslie.

It has the ring of truth. And it was obviously left purposely. One structure on a planet and one object inside. I think the Artonuee left behind the book as a history of their race. As a message to anyone who might come after they were gone.

Only the Artonuee?

Sir, since the structure housing the book withstood some considerable heat for a long period of time, since it was unlike anything described in the Artonuee culture, I think that leaving the book was a joint effort by the Artonuee and the Delanians.

Perhaps. But I see that our time is up. Tomorrow, we will study the next segment. Please reread it, keeping in mind our discussion of today. As you have already noted, no doubt, there is a change in viewpoint; before our discussion period begins, I will want you to consider why this was desirable. And give some thought, please, since this is a literature class, to the artistic integrity of the abrupt change of view. And one more request. Please remember my age, my young friends, and do not trample me on the way to the dining hall.

7

There was no sense of urgency. It was dreamlike, unreal; but no problem to Rei, for man conquers. Daily man vanquishes all the ills to which he is heir. He had that sort of confidence here. Where? Brown atmosphere. Sand. Water somewhere.

He was there and his friend was there. Who? There was a warm feeling of comradeship. They had to get the hell out of there, but they could do it.

There was a tunnel arrowing into blackness. It was lined with light. He went, confident, flying. The tunnel closed and filled. Huge forces shook him. His friend was gone, swallowed up by blackness. There was no face, only an awareness, a knowledge that his friend had surrendered.

Outside the tunnel the world was brown. There was water somewhere. The sky was there, but unseen.

He knew immediately that they were mother and daughter. The younger one was attractively slim with a multicolored soft fur for skin. The older one was woman with a trace of the hardness which sometimes comes with maturity, but still woman, convincing, alluring. They didn't speak. It was a long time before he heard them, but they were telling him.

"Come, come."

He was not ready.

With no sense of urgency he was in a long room. Ahead of him stretched stainless steel cases, boxes, all on legs to raise them to face- and chest-level. He understood that he was to progress from station to station. He stood before the first case, the line of steel enclosures perspecting away to the far end of the room where a man in a white lab coat puttered, clipboard in hand.

An automated hypodermic needle swung out from the steel and jabbed at him. He sensed, feared evil. He pushed. There was no sound as the case fell. He pushed, pushed, fighting now, for he knew that it was urgent. He knew this place. Case after case fell with no sound, crashing noiselessly, surprisingly fragile, dominoing case after case until, near the end of the long room, he stood in the shambles as the white-smocked man advanced, a long needle menacingly ready.

He ran. A door opened into a cul-de-sac, a molding, musty, cement-walled room of damp threat with corpses, and they were there, the two women, one young and full-lipped and beautiful, although strange, the other only slightly less beautiful but possessed of that warning hint of mastery.

They clung to him. He knew the woman-warmth was hypocrisy, far removed from reality, a force holding him through the engendered male response to femininity. The long, shining needle pierced his arm, going deep; no, his thigh. On each side. He was walking, one of them on either side, clinging, immobilizing his arms, leaving them to hang weakly as they moved timelessly across the brown with water somewhere and the sky not seen and they were thinking, feeling.

"Come, come."

There was the aura of cruelty about the mother, a beautiful and mature being. Her daughter, young, fresh, gave him something approaching empathy. She cared. She didn't like what she was doing, but it was the nature of things. There was something between them, him and the daughter, something indefinable. Her grasp was less possessive, less limpet-like.

He had to get away.

He could fly. By pumping his legs he built something, compressions, something, underneath. He went up. Three trees stood apart from the forest. The younger one seized on. He tried to dislodge her before the cruel one came.

"Come. Come."

She was almost gentle, but there was the older one, clamping onto his bare thigh, making herself one huge mouth which sucked, buried itself leech-like in the thin pad of flesh over his hip joint. Pain. Not blood being sucked but something more vital. They were bearing him down, weighting him, ending the flying. Almost reluctantly the young one ceased being a woman and became that leech-mouth feeding on something vital, digging hurtingly into the flesh over the opposite hip joint, and he was going, hearing them more clearly, although there were no words.

"Come. Come."

Brownness. Brown sand and water somewhere, and they were sapping him, the sucking maws obscene, evil, limpets clinging as if to wet rock, impossible to displace although his fingers dug and dug into his own skin and got a nailhold under the soft one, the young one who exuded that feeling of near empathy.

He did not want to go. He had things to do. She, the younger one, was also reluctant, not liking what she was doing to him. She was the weaker of the two, weaker than the sucking, strong, cruel mother-thing which made the brown come near with her enervating bite. He screamed in pain. His fingers dug until, with a sucking sound, the younger one let go and was in his hand, a thing, unidentifiable but alive and sinister, pulsing, red maw underneath.

No. He would not go. Man conquers. Man, all men, materialized in him, reminding him of his mission. With a final, wrenching effort, he displaced the other thing which had existed, once, in the guise of woman. The two things in his hands fought. He knew his time was short, measured in seconds, although all was time-

less as he forced the two sucking things maw to maw
and felt them shudder as mutual force destroyed them.
He had won.

He could fly again.

Lift under him, tired, not able to fly as he once
could fly, he saw the water underneath. The things
were melting, but still living. He could see their gory
hearts hanging like melting ice. The water was the
place for them, far out. But he could not make it. The
calm water was close. The younger one was thinking,
feeling. Her being alive terrified him.

"Come. Come."

He cast them, bound together by their own force,
into the smooth water, and then he was sinking. He fell
only feet from them. The shore was near. He swam. He
could hear the younger one calling.

"Come. Come."

Mindless.

Ahead of him in the smooth, perfumed water, was
the broad, flat back of a Bolun, familiar, ancient, kept
alive, some eons past, by love and daily medication.
Old, fine, loved pet. He put him to sleep, the finest Bolun in the system, and he cried. The Bolun knew what
was happening. After dozens of trips to the veter-
inarian, the Bolun knew what was happening, for he'd
never complained before, never wept that howling wail
before. The Bolun had struggled against needles and
rectum worm checks and parasite removal and all such
indignities, but he knew that this was more than just
one more needle. It wouldn't hurt going into the tough,
fight-scarred scruff of the neck, but the Bolun knew
that this was the final needle, and the world's finest Bolun howled because his friend didn't have the guts to
stay there and watch him die. Howl in his ears going
out the door with tears forming in his eyes, and ahead
of him in the perfumed water the broad, fat, black
back, swimming. How could it be? And the young
thing calling.

"Come. Come."

Far down the light-lined tunnel were the doors to the universe. He screamed and reached for them, his arm stretching, stretching, falling short. Inside those doors, warmth, love, safety.

"He got away."

"Who got away?"

"Him."

His hand went through the doors. All he ever wanted was inside, all of it there. Behind him the water. He turned his head and listened. A keening in his ears. Musical.

"Come. Come." The dark voice under the music.

He knew who he was not by name, not by identity, and there it all was behind him inside the doors, and he could open them, only his hand went through the doorknob, and out there were the things from which he'd escaped, and the water had not always been perfumed. The water was timeless until it began to boil and steam as a world died. The mad, grasping, deadly feel of it.

The brown coming back, misty, and he could no longer fly, and if the things were not to take him, then what? He had escaped to what?

8

To unbearable pain. To perfumed water being sprinkled on his lips. To fever and heat and a burning sun and drenching rains and endless pain and the taste of an alien sweetness as he opened his mouth, seeing his action from a distance, eyes closed, feeling it. A twittering, keening musical presence. Breeze fanned into his burning face and the festering of the terrible wound and the raw hurt of his hip joints and a weakness.

He screamed soundlessly, for he knew the room, the long, cold room with steel cabinets. The needles to draw fluid from lifeless bodies. The first expedition, racked by internal explosion, body parts strewn, the ship towed home and the parts gathered and boxed in steel cases and embalmed, since no one knew the force which destroyed them and autopsy was necessary.

His strong body fighting the wounds. Mind imprisoned. Fighting to be free, but weakened by the total war his cells fought against the infections. Boji, Boji, fat, black Bolun.

Perfumed water, pure, alien. And the alien sweetness. Mouth dry, swallowing. Body wastes accumulating. Unable to move. Stinking. Sun after sun.

"The goddamned sensors failed!" Terror. Feverish activity. The rumble of the engines.

Wham!

Soundless scream as walls buckled, compartments burst. The ring of impact at speed.

46

"Brake, Rei. Full brake."

Birds. No. Insects. Beautiful. Lovely eyes. Tiny. Twittering. Long, flexible lips on tiny faces. The sprinkle of sweetness.

And his body fighting, strong, healthy, fantastically versatile in healing itself. Endless suns and the cooling rain and the washing away of filth and the sound of children's voices fading into that tuneless, musical keening and wings beating like giant moths and a part of his mind alive, now.

He tried to focus his eyes. His lips moved. A croaking sound which stopped the musical twittering.

They were dead.

All of them, dead, and with them had died hope and the excitement of discovery. The first men to find an alien civilization and all dead. Free electrons floating on the surface of a sun.

It was clear. He could not see, but it was clear. The impact had ripped the engineering section, taking three men with the shattered bits of rock and metal which burst into free space. The panel erupting in his face, a long, hot sliver piercing him. Juanna screaming, "Suits!" Suits mandatory on planetary approach, but Juanna holed by a rock which penetrated the hull as if it were so much soft flesh, her blood spewing as she was exposed to hard vacuum.

The engines, the remaining port-side pair, screaming, failing as servos went with the rain of space debris. And the sun ahead. His suit patch, automated, holding. Bleeding inside the suit, the warm fluid sinking to his feet and wetting them until, with concentration, he closed the veins and hit the engines, screaming, "Start, damn you. Start."

Screaming into the dead communications system. "Engines!" No answer. A dimming scanner showing the gutted compartment and a smear of red on the jagged edge of the gaping hole in the hull.

The ship was dead. It shot past a small, sunside planet and the heat built as he armed the mechanical demo release of the escape hatch. His hands weak, trembling.

Then he was aspin in space, traveling the arc of the dying ship into the sun. Hope. He could tell them. Ah, the rotten luck of it. Valuable tools and equipment going into that goddamned sun. But they had the means to send a lightspeed message. There was hope. Five worlds there. Four life-zone worlds, packed closely around a fine, stable sun.

Nothing vital had been ruptured in the circuits of the suit and the backpack made sounds inside the suit, fighting the pull of the sun and winning, accelerating, as he browned out. Heat straining the capacity of the suit but cooling as the sun world swam past. And there would be, in a civilization which could beam messages into interstellar space, people on the second world.

After a long period of sleep he awoke with the wetness on his lips and looked into the multifaceted eyes of a tiny angel. Long, soft lips almost touched his, loosing the rain of sweetness. Tiny hands pushed the fruit into his lips. Around him they swarmed in dozens.

"Thank you," he said. The sound sent them skittering on a flare, leaving him alone. Had they, or he, lifted his visor?

God, he stank.

His left leg was useless. The abdominal wounds were scabbed over, healing. His head was clear.

Around him an empty world, the six-inch winged angels hovering at a distance. Across the water, trees, dense, thick-leaved. A part of his dream. Things crawled on the limbs.

"Come. Come."

He rested.

On a limb overhanging the lake something moved, jerked, pulsed. With a feeble hand he closed his visor. He thumbed magnification into it and watched, the hours meaningless, his body using the time to heal. The movement came from a rounded node on the limb, white, silken. And as hours flowed, a tiny hand emerged, clutched, rested, as he rested. A head. Wet antennae unfolded in the heat of the sun. A struggle. One of the winged angels, fully formed, sat, in exhaustion, on the limb. Wings wet, folded. Fascinated, he did not take his eyes off the tiny, beautiful creature until it flexed its drying wings, launched itself into air, fell, caught, soared, wings beating, keening voice singing a note of joy.

A world of butterflies. A goddamned world of bugs. Where were the people who sent the message?

His chronometer said that he'd been healing for fourteen standard days.

On the fifteenth day, he struggled out of the stinking, soiled suit, crawled to the water's edge. He checked it carefully. But he'd been in that water. It was unhospitable to the sucking things which crawled the trees and munched leaves on the other side of the lake. He pulled himself in, bathed, discarding his clothing, letting the perfumed water cool his burning, scabbed wounds.

His movements frightened the tiny winged creatures. No longer did they bring him food. At a distance, he watched them, saw among them creatures, less delicate, unwinged, who walked the ground on two legs, much like men.

He had swum ashore to a grassy knoll. From the top, gained by much effort, pulling his still mending leg behind him, he could see a plain of flowers. The flowers were alive with the winged angels.

He could not get far from water, not in his condition. But he had to have food. Apparently, the angels had fed him their own food, nectar. He grinned, his face feeling crackly under his fifteen-day beard. Kept alive for fifteen days by a bunch of bugs feeding him flower juice.

He reached the near flowers. They smelled sweet and the nectar was a cluster of grains, pulpy, in the stamen. He ate. Around him the angels twittered and seemed to laugh.

"Good," he said to them, scattering them. "Very good. You live quite the life, don't you?"

The flowers, themselves, offered more bulk and were quite tasty.

In the evening he sat on top of the knoll. The angels circled him at a distance. He waved to them, motioned them to come closer. One, with a head larger than the others, a head so heavy that she flew rather clumsily, approached. He made motions to his mouth. They had to have some intelligence to know that he required food to live, water to survive. They'd kept him alive. The angel with the large head twittered and keened. He repeated the eating motions.

She had tiny hands, perfectly formed. Her legs, tucked up, seemed less well formed. They had given him something other than flower nectar. He made the motions. He started to speak, but remembered that the sound of his voice frightened them. He'd seen the fruit on the large trees across the lake. He pointed, shaped his hands in the circle of the fruit, motioned.

The angel keened, flew heavily across the water. Others followed. It took three of them, working together, to bring a whole fruit. They placed it a few yards away and retreated. He crawled to it. Ate with relish. The fruit was good. The juice ran down his chin. He motioned again and the same three angels brought a second fruit. He smiled, waved. He took the second fruit and crawled back down the hill. The chill of evening was upon him. He crawled into the suit and slept.

He awoke with the sun in his eyes and they were there, at the top of the knoll. Some of the wingless ones carried a shapeless mass, placed it there on the smooth grass. He crawled to it. It was flesh, but flesh of a sort he'd never seen. He tasted it cautiously. It was spicy, chewy. Yet it was new. He ate the fruit, left the flesh. He'd been fantastically lucky. The flower food and the fruit were compatible with his system. The flesh was strange. He withdrew to bathe in the lake. The wingless ones came to the flesh and, gesturing, ate of it. Finding that he'd had no ill effects from the bite he'd sampled that morning, he tried some of it for lunch, ate hungrily.

By the twentieth day, the large-headed angel would approach to within a few feet of him, stand erect on her legs, which seemed to be developing, and twitter at him. Her head was growing. Now she was so heavy that she walked, instead of flying.

He was able to make the link between the crawling things of the trees and the winged angels. Butterflies in metamorphosis. The round, mawed things the larvae, the rounded sac the chrysalis—the sac he'd observed as it gave birth to a fully formed angel. But this change which took place from day to day in his large-headed friend with the feminine features, the large eyes, the cute, protruding rear? After perfection, what?

When he was able, after twenty-five days, to limp on his leg, the flowered plain drew him, led him away from the lake, water stored in his suit-pack. He carried fruit and a hunk of the spicy flesh. He traveled slowly. Ahead were low hills and beyond, mountains. He walked through a grove of the thick-leaved trees and looked warily for the crawling larvae. Apparently there was some natural boundary, some natural rule. Only the winged angels and the walking ones, looking much like tiny men, watched his passage. The trees supplied him with fruit.

His large-headed friend paced him. Flying now and then, walking tiredly most of the time. She was growing visibly and flying became more and more difficult for her as the third day of his journey took him past clear, perfumed streams and groves of the fruited trees. They seemed to know no season; young pips of fruit mixed with maturing and ripened fruit on the same branch.

He was following the sun. It led him up steep hills to the crest of the low range and before him was the sea and there, far below, was movement. He used the magnifier in his visor and saw them, angels, grown large, wings tiny on their backs.

Steep cliffs ran along the shore. The descent to them was tortuous. The large-headed angel glided down on the updrafts, body ungainly in flight, too big for flight. He, being a mere man, had to walk, crawl, slide.

A wind came off the sea into his face. There was a perfume in it. And, using his magnifier, he saw that the sea was not an ocean. There, on the far horizon, was land.

Around him, the angels, all grown, wings dwarfed, heads heavy, twittered, seemed to ignore him. They were few in numbers, so few that he thought he could identify his traveling companion. Grown to the size of a ten-year-old child, she was preening herself. The delicate, multicolored fur shredded away. He watched with amazement as she seemed to expand, to grow.

Nearby, the process of molting completed, an angel launched herself off the cliff. She was so large that her tiny wings could not possibly hold her; he thought she had leaped to her death, far below in the waves which pounded the rocks, pushed by the constant wind. But she steadied in her downward flight, circled, soared, wings almost motionless, riding the updraft and then gliding off on a wing toward the distant land.

Head large, eyes glowing, his friend pushed down the last remnant of her outer skin, kicked it aside. He'd seen women take off a skirt with identical motions.

"Wait; please wait," he called.

She did not look at him, her eyes fixed on the distant land. And, as he moved toward her, she was gone. Falling, then feeling the updraft, gliding, impossibly heavy for such flight, but flying, soaring, becoming small in the distance.

There was no food on the barren shore. The water, if it were fresh, was far below. He climbed the hill, found food, running water, and spent the days sitting on the hilltop, watching as the angels molted, leaped, soared.

It took two weeks, fourteen standard days, for the angel, the newly changed Artonuee female, to develop her powers of communication to the point where she could tell of the strange male who escaped the ifflings and fed on nectar and fruit and the flesh food of the walking males.

9

"We know, dear," said First Mother Piiree, when, with much agitation and self-pleasure, the third-change infant formed her first coherent message in a keening mixture of sweet sounds and labored thoughts. "Concern yourself with the application of the sound eeeeen. Now, now, he is well. He is being watched. He is feeding." Lovely, thought First Mother Piiree, to be fortunate enough to share these lovely children's first odd and ancient joys. Unfortunate that this group of changelings should have had their wingling stage complicated by the presence of the alien. The trauma of it could color their future lives, and the life of each was a precious jewel to be treasured, protected. Now that the three pleasant worlds of the Artonuee were population-stabilized, the flow of changelings through the Development Center was slow and carefully regulated.

There were times when Piiree wished that she had lived during the period of expansion, when the Artonuee were peopling new worlds. She herself had voted, at the last Public Opinion, to expand Five, cold as it was. She had argued against the quality-of-life advocates, stating with some force that she knew from her personal experience and her graduate research that a one-on-one relationship at the iffling stage was no more desirable than multiple relationships. The age of expansion, she had said, should prove to even the most skeptical that the life force was powerful enough to give being to two, three, even as many as five ifflings. The great Lonwee was a fiveling. It was a terrible waste to allow only one iffling the gift of advancement when an Artonuee came home.

Just last night she had talked about it with the Lady from Nirrar. "It is not as if we are denying them life," the Lady said. "We are merely postponing it. Look at it this way. In our mythology, the Lady Andee suckled fifty ifflings. Each became great. I agree that it is possible to advance more than one or two ifflings with each homecoming, but is it desirable? Part of our history is the sad story of the age of overpopulation, of rampant changeling mortality. Rather than condoning artificial concern with unfertilized eggs and unadvanced ifflings I, personally, would advise a continuation of careful control, of watchfulness, of Artonueeistic benevolence in regard to those who are allowed the gift of sentient life."

The Lady was high in the government, and in her position, had access to information unavailable to Piiree. She bowed. Moreover, the Lady was carrying a wing load of sorrow. It registered there around her eyes, in the sad purse of her lovely lips.

"Your load is heavy, Lady," Piiree said, in consideration. "I will allow you to retire, with just one more question. The meaning of the alien's presence on The World, Lady?"

For an unguarded moment, there was a chaos of thought, then the Lady controlled herself. "Great change, First Mother. For good or for ill. At best, your wishes granted in a staggering surplus." Pictures of thousands, millions of changelings. An outflowing of changelings to live great and exciting lives of—Piiree was lost.

"I will wish for it," Piiree said, leaving the chamber as the tired Lady, clad in official purple, keened goodnight.

Still, Piiree resented the presence of the alien, the male. He sat, a malignancy in paradise, atop the Cliffs of Flight, eating the fruit which properly belonged to the trekking changelings. Piiree had a healthy respect for the ability of the male of the species, as long as he stayed in his place. This alien male was definitely out of his place. She was glad, after so many days of suspense and anxious watching, that the government had, at last, sent someone to deal with the situation. All she wanted was for the alien to be removed so that her changelings would not have, as one of their first memories, the image of him in their minds.

Behind her, the Lady could not sleep. To one who knew her, a dullness of eye, there in the outer facets, would have told of her fatigue, and of other things. To a soul mate—one who could, upon invitation, come into her head—all would have been revealed and then tears would have fallen, for the Lady had sacrificed much to be on The World, to hear the eager, childish voices of the changelings, to smell the drift of the aroma of the pleele flowers and the juplee forests across the inland sea. The pleele smell saddened her most.

Sleepless, she activated the darkened arcs and, from her carry case, extracted papers and leaned over them as she sat in her bed. Her lips formed sounds, unnatural sounds, guttural and strange and, although systematized, wounding to her ears still. And some of the sounds were incapable of being formed by her frail vocal chords. Some had to be thought, motioned. This gave her doubt. The mind which was the target of these sounds was unknown. Would her mixture of thought and sounds make sense to it?

It was an old worry and she had to live with it for yet a few hours, until the dawn and after the floater trip across the inland sea. And if she could not communicate, then it had all been for nothing. She felt a wave of unaccustomed bitterness.

No. She would not be able to bear failure. She would not even think of failure, not after the long days of work and the sleepless nights and the frightful psychic pain which still, in unguarded moments, smote her with a hurtful blow.

Still, there was the possibility of failure. For the first time in history, the Artonuee were exposed to the concept of linguistics, a term which she herself had coined in the first dramatic days of her study of the alien messages in that section of the Research Quad which had been turned over to her. The Artonuee, of course, had always had language. The libraries of Outworld were filled with the written word of the Artonuee, going back, in the ancient picture form of the language, over three hundred thousand Artonuee years to the days of the first tool users. But even in that early, rudimentary form of the language there was no difficulty, for the written pictures were merely graphic transcriptions of the pictures of the mind. It was thought in University circles that a primitive Artonuee female, from the early days of self-spun nests, would be able to converse with a modern-day Artonuee in basic terms, leaving out the additions to the language caused primarily by technological development.

It was true that in the era of the attempted space communications experiments, some thought had been given to the possibility that another intelligent race, out among the stars, would have different sounds in communication, even different ways of making communicative sounds. Yet the early language scientists—if such a title could, indeed, be bestowed upon those who formulated the messages to be sent into space—assumed that mind pictures of universal things, moons, stars, suns, words, people, would be universally understood. So it was that the interstellar messages were sent in primitive Artonuee picture writing.

And so it was that the answers were in basic pictures and, thus, easily understandable. That is, the first answers were in basic pictures, and the newest Artonuee changeling would have been able to see that the pictures indicated a sentient being of a race having two sexes and having young of the same form. From there it was easy. The system of numbers fell into place with a quickness which pleased Miaree. Within days she was able to determine that the speed of the Delanian rays of light was, on a scale accurate to the fifth decimal point, exactly the value of God's Constant, thus, the speed of light. In another day she knew and reported that the elements of the Delanian periodic table corresponded almost exactly with those of the Artonuee table, with some notable exceptions in the heavy metal end.

So far she was dealing with pictures and with numbers. It was when she waded into the stacked pages of duppaper dealing with language that she ran into problems. In one of her early reports, she illustrated her difficulty by enclosing a copy of an illustration from a Delanian message. Having mastered the Delanian alphabet, she was able to translate the words with the picture of a band of colors. It was labeled *The Visible Spectrum*. It was composed of waves measuring from 760 millimicrons to 385 millimicrons, and the band itself was labeled with meaningless names: *Red, White, Green, Blue. Violet.*

The finding had to do with more than language. In her report she wrote: It is obvious that the Delanian eye is an imperfect instrument with limited capability; this basic difference in the structure of a sense organ will make communication difficult, if not impossible, in matters pertaining to the wavelengths of light. Since there is such a basic difference in the physical make-up of this one important sense organ, it is to be assumed that other basic differences will also be present. In this specific instance, how can an Artonuee with diapasonic sight explain what she sees to a being with limited vision?

She was to find, as she plowed into the technical material, that, although Delanians could not see other wavelengths, they knew of their existence and could measure them with instruments, so that minor difficulty was overcome, but there were others.

Since Delanians saw light differently, she theorized, they would have an entirely different concept of the universe. Such thinking revealed to her one of the basic rules of language, while demolishing the common-language theories of the scientists who had worked on the communications project. She quickly learned that there is no relationship, in alien languages, between any label and the object for which it stands. There was no similarity between the Delanian and Artonuee words for star, for example.

The smaller figure in the three-person picture was called by various names: boy, son, young man, youth. There was no equivalent for any of those terms in the Artonuee language.

As the days passed and the beautiful unrest grew in her body, she began to understand the overwhelming task which awaited her. In desperation, she turned to the sound tapes which had been transmitted from the Delanian driver approaching the system. She had listened, briefly, before, had had her ears jarred by static and by the unmusical, growling, offensive sounds of the Delanian voice. Slowly, painfully, she began to relate the sounds to the Delanian alphabet, for the early broadcasts were, again, language lessons for beginners. And just as she put two sounds together and got star ship for driver, she knew that she would have to put aside the research.

Inside her slim body the eggs were forming, and as she worked, the chemical changes in her body imitated in smell the sweet, potent aroma of the pleele. The most glorious adventure of an Artonuee female called her. She dreamed of the love parks of Outworld. Artonuee males, in the Quad, catered to her, bowed to her, followed her. Small bouquets of pleele appeared on her desk, placed by male assistants, by males with whom she had never come into personal contact. On her brief outings into the city, males would pause, smile, keen a greeting, for she had not loosed her wings from her garment, had not displayed the sign that she had chosen, and in the ancient tradition, she was looking.

The attentions she received were her due. It was the right of any male to state his case. And yet, it interfered with her work and left her breathless and expectant, and she found herself wasting valuable time watching the flex of the leg muscles of the young male who served her needs in her personal office, lifting, carrying, running.

It was her right, as a young female feeling the strength of nature's call to fertilization, to freetime. Special transportation awaited her and her chosen. Outworld called. There the entire landscape had been modeled after The World's mating parks. There the planet was devoted to love and the creation of life and beauty. There the artistic minds of the four habitable worlds gathered and created music and the magic of words and objects of delight and there the lovers strolled and kissed and . . .

She had already been robbed of a part of it. She had planned her method of selection, from among the artists of Outworld, for she wanted her eggs to carry the seeds of beauty. She should have been on Outworld for weeks, selecting, rejecting, choosing. Her body cried out for love. It was ready, and hours of joy had been stolen from her by the hateful sounds of the Delanian voice on the sound tapes. She would endure no longer.

Yet, when she sent her application for freetime, it was not returned automatically. She had sent her physician's certificate, telling of her readiness, of her sacrifice in staying with the project to date. Yet the automatic approval did not come. Instead, an official courier brought an oral summons.

She had never known that so many handsome males walked the streets of Nirrar. She had never known that the male smile could be so pleasing.

"Lady," said the roller driver who took her to the Government Quad, "I know it is chill, but either I open the viewer or I faint."

The musky smell of pleele filled the compartment. She smiled and nodded.

The members of the guard were so beautiful they took her breath away. Tall, handsome, strong. They shone in their uniforms like beacons on the road to joy. And, superbly disciplined, they didn't turn a hair, although, as she wafted past, the delicious smell of pleele perfumed the air, leaving behind the slim, graceful lady a lingering, wistful sadness.

"Mother," she said, without waiting. "I must go. I must. There is so little time."

There was a sadness in Mother Aglee's eyes. They were alone in the Mother's office. Mother Aglee did not speak. Instead, she handed Miaree a packet.

"No, no," Miaree said. "I will not look."

"Open it, daughter," Mother Aglee said sadly.

It was, of course, the alien. Duppaper pictures, taken from afar with the long lens of an optical recorder.

"No, no," Miaree keened.

"You were making splendid progress," Mother Aglee said. "It was felt that no additional pressures were needed."

"Someone else will have to take over. There are my notes."

"You have the mind for it, daughter. You are one in a million."

"He survived all this time?" Miaree asked, feeling an interest in spite of the torturing storm in her mind, in her body.

"On The World. He was there three days before the disturbance in the thought flow alerted us. He was gravely injured."

"And you didn't pick him up immediately?"

Mother Aglee smiled. "Would our physicians have known how to heal him? Look."

Miaree saw the terrible wound, scabbed. She saw the broken, useless limb. "He is made from the same stuff, but his flesh is different," Mother Aglee said. "He loosed two ifflings, forced them from him, survived."

"No one looses an iffling," Miaree said. "He is different."

"He was healing when we found him. He was being fed by winglings, and nectar and fruit and flesh seemed to allow him to thrive. We thought to move him and submit him to the artificial foods of the adults could be worse than leaving him. The climate was mild. The rains tended to cleanse him. He is possessed of a powerful body with some unknown means of healing itself. We thought that his nature, even on an alien world, would know more than we. But now he is healed. He awaits on the Cliffs of Flight. Once he attempted to swim the island sea, and we feared that we would have to save him before you were ready, but he quickly saw the impossibility of swimming against the wind and the currents and turned back."

"Mother, I am not ready. I know barely two words of his language. I cannot communicate."

"That is why, my daughter, I must ask you to make the ultimate sacrifice."

Weakened, shocked, Miaree sat heavily.

"He is disturbing the wakening ids of the changelings, but that is a small matter. He grows impatient, but that, too, is not our concern. We received this," Mother Aglee said, handing over a single duppaper, "only yesterday. I would like you to confirm my impressions."

Miaree looked, and, with sinking heart, nodded. "Yes," she said, with dull resignation. "It means what you think."

The pictures showed a fleet of Delanian drivers moving through space in stylized simplicity. An inset showed the inside of a driver. Many Delanians, males, females, young.

Mother Aglee smiled weakly. "The fact that we have not invited them to visit us in such numbers seems irrelevant. I see this fleet as a threat. You know that we are limiting the advancement of ifflings to mere replacements. Now our worlds are pleasant. We have room to breathe and walk and the leisure to fly. What will our people say if they are told that they must share our life, our good worlds, with thousands of aliens? What is the rate of population growth with these aliens? How strong are they? Will they ask, or will they demand? Can we say no or will we be forced?"

"No, no," Miaree said, absorbing the words, but thinking, very privately, of herself. "Oh, no."

"My daughter," Mother Aglee said, standing, moving to put a soft hand on Miaree's shoulder. "We must talk with this alien. We must find out all we can about his people. How I wish I could say, 'Look, the fleet will not be here for a year; go to Outworld, daughter, and love.' But I cannot. Judging from the messages and the time element with the first driver, we cannot take that risk. It is the future of our race, of our system that we face, Miaree. I must ask. Yes, I have no choice. I must."

"I understand," Miaree said.

The simple operation was performed by the best doctors in the most modern hospital in the system. Lady Jonea was by her side. The Mother, herself, greeted her when she awoke from the mild, induced sleep.

"Miaree," Mother Aglee said, with deep emotion. "Oh, my daughter."

And from inside her, from an emptiness, came a vast, keening wail.

10

"Animals," she gasped, when she finally got the meaning. "They are animals."

"An interesting word," said her assistant, Lady Belfae. "A word out of prehistory."

"Their young are . . ." She hesitated, searching for an Artonuee word. "Changed alive. They are ripped from the mother's body alive."

"Animals," agreed Lady Belfae.

It was the only analogy. The early writings told of them. Small, scurrying things on the old World, things which preyed on the unhatched eggs of the Artonuee. Things which, in self-defense, they exterminated.

She was healed. The operation left no scars. It had merely removed her unfertilized eggs artificially. But there was a scar inside, on her mind.

She hated them, the Delanians. Loathesome, animalistic, ugly.

Not true. Not ugly.

Before her, to help her understand, were pictures. The alien at rest, walking, moving, undressed showing his maleness, standing on the Cliffs of Flight looking out over the inland sea. Not ugly. Tall, powerful, graceful in his way. Not much thicker in torso than an Artonuee male and possessed of the same general features, although his eyes were small and his legs longer, seemingly made for the covering, in a short time, of vast distances.

But not ugly.

And, in all fairness, it was his evolution which determined that he would be ripped alive from his mother's body like an animal.

"'That there is evolution is undeniable," a consultant told her. "Fossil remains show us our ancestors, incredibly ancient, small, ill-formed, brains the size of a jenk seed. And there are other evidences. The forms of the exterminated animals of the old World changed over the ages. In defense of your alien, I wonder what the ages would have done to the animals if we had not destroyed them?"

"He is an intelligent being," she told herself, listening to a voice on the tapes, the grating sounds no longer so painful. "In many ways he must be superior to us, at least in technology, for he has traveled the stars. I must give him his due. I must approach him as an equal."

And, when she could think in Delanian, although that term was no longer relevant, since she now knew the names with which the aliens labeled themselves, she told herself that she was ready. She had learned much.

The existence of two sexes was more important to the Delanians than to the Artonuee. Language was feminine in the Artonuee system. The Delanians differentiated in their language. Hers and his were the same, only different. Since there was no evidence of being able to share thoughts among the Delanians, their language was far more complicated. Concepts which were expressed among the Artonuee with one quick picture—perhaps, in some cases, combined with sound—required long, complicated, roundabout explanation in the words of the Delanians.

It was only with the help of the Research Quad main computer and through long, hard hours of concentration that she was able to board the driver to The World with some confidence that she would be able to converse intelligently with the alien.

And on the night prior to the meeting, there was still

some doubt in her mind. She tried to master it. Then she tried to sleep with that aching loneliness inside her, that feeling of loss. She awoke irritable, feeling the effect of planet change. On New World, she would be in the middle of a work day. Here at home—this merely a phrase, since she had not seen the surface of The World since her days as a changeling—it was dawn. The sun was warmer, more friendly. As it began to light the darkness, it seemed to be more powerful, dimming the evil fire of the collisions in its brilliance. She bowed to the shrine provided in each guest room.

"Be with me, Mother." The prayer was brief, but in a very real way, her very thoughts were a continuation of her supplication. Perhaps the priests of her youth were right. Perhaps it was possible for God to forgive. Old Jarvel, senior member of the male minority in the Interplanetary Council, called in to hear the astounding news that the Artonuee were not alone in facing God's Fires, paled, fell to his knees.

"They are God's messengers," old Jarvel said, spittle running down his chin. He was long overdue for his homecoming, but his importance as the leading spokesman for Artonuee males seemed, somehow, to put renewed life into his ancient carcass. "If it is indeed true that they have bested God's Constant, that must be construed as a sign."

When he had gone, however, the Lady Jonea, with a wry smile, said, "Or it is a sign that God, all along, has been largely in the minds of the Artonuee."

Cynicism seemed to increase with age in a female, Miaree observed.

But she did not voice her hopes in prayer to the shrine. Instead, she paid lip service to God and, as she robed herself in purple, wings hidden in modesty, she indulged in an if-you-are-really-there soliloquy. If you are really there you must be God of the Delanians, too, for our concept of an omnipotent God is incompatible with the idea that another race in our own galaxy would find a different God. It was, she felt, an all-or-nothing thing. Either God was God of all the universe or was God of nothing. And, even more daringly, if God were God of the Artonuee alone, then Her power was limited and therefore subject to dispute.

The males said that the seeds of atheism were in every female and that the very act of flying was in defiance of God. So, she decided, since she had been fighting God all her life, she would now carry with her across the inland sea a will to fight harder than ever, to use the chink in God's armor—namely the fact that the Delanians had traveled in space at multiples of light speed—to destroy God's last hold over the Artonuee. With the help of the Delanians' vast power, that power which blinked with the forces of a living sun, she would rescue the life force of the Artonuee from the doom which, as the sun burned through a morning ground haze, dimmed into insignificance in the bright, daytime sky.

"Mother Piiree," she said, having finished her breakfast which included the rare treat of ripe juplee fruit, "you may tell the workers that I am ready."

The small floater, with two young and curious males as crew, flew before the wind which blew, ever constant, toward the Cliffs of Flight. The sea was white-capped. The unaccustomed motion, however, could not break through Miaree's concentration as she rehearsed her welcoming speech to the man from the Constellation of Delan. The floater's storage cells fed on the energy of the sun, pushed the floater with pumped jets of water, hummed quietly. The wind cooled her, fluttered her purple robe. Overhead, a female changeling soared, ungainly on her tiny wings, ignoring the floater as she sped across the waters to her destiny. And ahead, the cliffs rose from the sea, tall, barren, harsh.

The alien had shed his bulky space suit and was standing on a high crag, eyes shaded against the morning sun.

The landing point was a distance to his right. He noted the direction of the boat, walked along the top of

11

And so much, my young friends, for interplanetary diplomacy. Or was it, Stella, the most propitious thing that Rei could have said?

I think it was sweet.

Your powers of expression overwhelm me. A male viewpoint, please. Tomax?

I have to commend Rei for his patience. After all, he was nearly killed in the asteroid belt, narrowly escaped falling into the Artonuee sun. He lay in a stinking space suit with his own wastes for days, severely wounded. He has had nothing to eat but butterfly food for—how long? Over fifty days. In that position I might not feel like being formal and diplomatic.

Elizabeth.

He is a man and his response to Miaree's greeting is quite manlike, quite condescending. I think it was an insult.

Yes, LaConius.

I think it was merely an honest reaction to Miaree. I would think she'd be pleased.

It is, isn't it, a rather minor question? Let us review the segment of the fable which we've read together today. The most impressive aspect, John?

I'm intrigued by the continued mention of the art planet of Outworld.

Naturally. Leslie?

I would have liked more detail on Miaree's work in learning the Delanian language.

An interesting aspect. Some thoughts on language, Clear Thought the Healer?

In our legends there is mention that the old ones spoke in many tongues. It is a concept which says much. It rather staggers the imagination. I know something of the difficulty of learning a language, although I have some advantage. Being able to communicate in mind pictures makes it unnecessary for the old race to know words, but in practice we have found it advantageous to use our tongues rather than our minds. We know the rules of privacy, as legislated following the reconciliation. In cases of emergency, or with permission, I am allowed to enter a mind. Otherwise, I speak. And I can understand Miaree's problems. One picture is worth many words; able to communicate with what apparently is a mixture of telepathy and sounds, she is handicapped in her contact with the alien by having to use his words. She has observed, or the writer has observed, that one simple concept which could be flashed instantly mind-to-mind takes a circuitous route through the maze of Delanian words.

Thank you, Clear Thought, you do very well with our primitive language. Without stating it is a concept that you must accept simply because I state it, I would like to observe that we are deficient in the field of language. I sometimes wonder if the universal language law should have been passed. We stem, of course, from a common source, all of us, from the rim worlds to the outposts toward the center. But as the centuries passed, as worlds became more isolated and independent from the parent civilization around Terra II, we began to develop variations in language. New materials, new life forms, new concepts on a hundred different worlds created words which had meaning only in one specific area of the empire. Accents changed. Although it never reached the point where one man could not understand another, there was a different ring in the ear when one conversed, for example, with a rimmer and with a center worlder. A child from the rim might say mumu as his first word, while a toddler from the center would say mama. Planetary influences changed speech. I once met a man from Big. That, incidentally, is a beautiful example of descriptive naming. Big is a giant planet in the second arm which circles its sun with astounding slowness. Men are born and die before one Big year is complete. My friend from Big told me that the planet's leisurely plodding through space has influenced its peoples. And, indeed, he spoke so slowly. One wanted to help him, put words into his mouth. He made a two-syllable word out of now. Yet, aside from the drawling sound of his words, his pronunciation is much like yours or mine. We have acknowledged our interdependency. Although we have armaments which can kill a planet, we have not used them since the War with Zede II. We number in the billions and yet we are alone. We still have our alarmists who cite the dead worlds to justify our so-called preparedness or the continued production of weapons of destruction. Perhaps this vague outside threat is what helps hold us together. We are, in spite of our far-flung travels, one people. And the lengths to which we have gone to keep it that way, among them the enforcement of the standard language regulations, are for the good. Except, as in the case of the Miaree manuscript, when we run into something totally new and different. I have read that the computers used in translating this small book ran continuously for eleven years before one single key was found. The number of problems presented to the computers was astronomical. The final solution is required study for programmers to the present date. If you think Miaree was astounding in her ability to decipher the Delanian language, think what a task she would have faced had not the Delanians sent pictures, the alphabet, carefully-thought-out keys to their language. But my point is this. By killing initiative in the creation of new language, by smoothing over the language of a galaxy, we left ourselves without a science of linguistics and faced a grave challenge when the Miaree manuscript was brought home from Cygnus. Now I am sure that, somewhere out there, there are others. Someday we will meet them. An alien race can be warlike or peaceful. We will have to assess their intentions rapidly, when we meet them. If we came face to face with the planet-killers and one of them said, 'stand or I fire!' we would not, of course, have time to learn language. We would have to make a spot assessment of his intentions and fire or be fired upon; however, I think that contact will not be sudden and unexpected, but will come, as it came to Miaree, with advance warning. And, thanks to Miaree and her book, we now have the capacity to study and solve an alien language in a mere fraction of the time it took to translate the legend. So you see, the study of literature is not just entertainment, is it?

Sir, there are other languages. The language of the eye. It spoke to Rei when Miaree came to him. It spoke in the form of beauty. And it is established that Miaree does not consider Rei ugly, although he is different.

Ah, John, the eye of the artist, eh? Yes, and the language of movement. There are certain signs which would be universal to an intelligent being. But the wormfly of Omaha III was beautiful before it was exterminated. It had lovely red wings and a soft, furry body and the early settlers considered it harmless, even beneficial, until they learned that in its breeding stage it carefully numbed the skin of its human victims and injected rather nasty little parasites which delighted in feeding on the tissue of the inner eye. And it is said the women of Zede II were beautiful beyond compare. Yet they formed the suicide fleet and almost broke through the blockade into the undefended worlds. Question. Any comment on the manner of Rei's escape from his dying ship? LaConius?

Rather simple, sir. A rocket pack on his space suit. Evidently just enough power to take him to the New

World—no, I mean The World, the original planet. I was a bit confused, at first, by the initial sequence, but it became clear when I got the picture of how the Artonuee develop. It is, as I said, very much like the Tigian butterfly, with an initial stage, the egg; a larval stage, the iffling; a stage of chrysalis, the sac which Rei saw hatching a wingling; and a butterfly stage, the winglings, before the final change into the semi-adult Artonuee. I presume the males follow much the same pattern, but since this book was written by an Artonuee female, the males get short shrift.

The room with the steel cabinets, Elana?

It's explained. It was sort of a funeral hall. Or a medical hall where victims of some space accident were brought. Evidently Rei was there at the time and was much impressed, for his dream of death and the room came, I'd guess, from his subconscious while he was trying to fight off the ifflings.

How do you feel about the ifflings? Martha?

Rather crawly. But I was impressed by Miaree's repugnance toward the so-called animal method of birth. I suppose, to a butterfly, with its clean and non-bloody laying of eggs, live birth would seem as horrible as the concept of giving poor old Beafly, still alive, to the cannibalistic ifflings.

Do the ifflings eat flesh, then? Julius?

No. I don't think so. I got the idea that they were just taking something intangible—the life force, as it were.

Comment, Alfred.

I think they'd have to take the Artonuee equivalent of genes, or at least DNA messengers. Because it is apparent that the activity of the early forms of the Artonuee stems from instinctive knowledge rather than learned knowledge. And I got a hint, in the Rei sequence, that there is some sort of continuous line of awareness running through all of the Artonuee. The ifflings which were fastened to Rei seemed to have some form of thought, at least enough for him to sense that they were female. A younger one and an older one.

And why were the ifflings female, Cecile?

Coincidence, maybe. Or, perhaps, controlled coincidence, since the female of the species seems to be dominant and more aggressive. It could be concluded from the state of the society that since the adult females are the stronger, the ifflings carrying female genes or whatever would also be stronger, more aggressive, more likely to tackle an unfamiliar form of life.

Yes, Alaxender.

I think it's interesting to find that the two life forms, Artonuee and Delanian, are so compatible that the ifflings could attack Rei's life force.

A good point, and one which could have bearing on the relationship between Rei and Miaree. Now, a quick summation. Overall impressions. Leslie.

I think the most important fact which is presented—

Fact, Leslie?

Idea, then. I think it's quite impressive that the Artonuee galaxy should have two intelligent life forms.

But was it the Artonuee galaxy? Could not the Delanians have come from the colliding galaxy?

No, because the pictures showed their planet to be in a constellation long known by the Artonuee.

I am not saying that you are wrong, Leslie. No one can say that you're wrong. It is a question that still interests some of our best minds. It has a bearing on the origin of life throughout the universe. Let me put it this way. A race with the capacity of star travel could have moved into the Artonuee galaxy from the colliding galaxy. There is a theory that some unknown controlling force in each galaxy determines the direction of life.

But, sir, the Dead Worlds—

Ah, yes, Tomax, the Dead Worlds. Definitely nonhumanoid. So different, so alien that a thousand studies have produced almost as many possible descriptions of the inhabitants. Actually, I mentioned the one-race theory to test you. We have proof, in our own galaxy, that two very dissimilar races can develop. So, I am not saying that the Artonuee and the Delanians were from different galaxies. I am merely mentioning that it is possible that the Delanians could have moved into the Artonuee galaxy from the rim of the colliding galaxy. But I agree with Leslie that it is a fascinating idea to think that one galaxy could produce two intelligent life forms. And that brings up an interesting question. Why are we so all-fired interested in contacting another intelligent race? Are we, like Artonuee females, still undecided about God? Do we need contact with another race, with a different background, to say, 'Hey, old fellow, about God...'

Tomorrow then, my young friends. I understand that we're having Vegan steak, eh?

12

She stood with her delicate feet slightly apart, left foot advanced. Her feet were bare. One toe curled nervously. The purple silk gown moved lightly in the on-shore wind, caressing her articulated ankles. The gown clung to narrow shoulders, bulged gracefully over folded wings, and the color showed through the thin material, iridescent blues, muted yellows. A pulse beat in her long, slender neck. The gossamer fur of her upper torso, exposed by the cut of the gown, was a lovely mixture of colors. And her eyes. Her eyes were the stars of the night, captured in individual facets in deep blue. Her face, ovate, delicate, showed that formal little smile. He answered it with a broad grin, showing white teeth.

"Those," he said, pointing to graceful antennae which sprouted from her forehead above the inner reaches of each eye, "are they sense organs?"

"They measure waves of the length of . . ."

He shook his head. Her speech reminded him of the music of home. But her attempts at the technical words left something to be desired.

"Forgive me," he said. "I am Rei, Captain of the Fleet. Native of . . ." To her, there was a gap, the strange sound losing itself on her ears. "I come in peace and friendship. I bring best greetings from the Council of Worlds and our Joint Leaders. We come from—"

"We call it the constellation Delan."

76

"I like the sound."

"I extend the apologies of our worlds for having left you alone so long. It was felt—"

"That the alien knew more about healing himself than you?"

She lidded her eyes, paying compliment to his understanding. The soft velvet of her lids was an extension of her beauty. She was, to Rei, a lovely thing out of a fairy tale. A creature of sugar and delicate silken threads.

"You are female," he said.

"Yes," she said, in Artonuee.

"Yes," he repeated. "A beautiful language."

"The sound is made thus," she said, repeating it for him. "High in the mouth."

"There is a thickness to my tongue," he said.

"There is time for learning," she said. "Now, we must go. A place has been prepared for us."

She led the way. He followed down the crude, carved steps. In the small floater, he had to sit close to her.

"My companions were killed," he said, as the floater pushed against the wind with silent force.

"It is sad."

"The fleet," he said. "Have they contacted you?"

She glanced at him, her eyes turning a deeper shade of blue. Was it the light? He was to learn, later, that her eyes were reflections of her emotions.

"They send messages. The messages disturb us."

"I can understand," he said. He was beginning to realize that some of the sounds were unheard when she spoke. Interesting. Yet he understood. "We come as uninvited guests. But you must know from what we flee."

"Yes. We call them God's Fires."

"You understand our plight, then."

"Are there not other worlds?"

"You are in space," he replied.

She was silent. To reveal the lack of star flight in her technology would be to admit a weakness.

"At the moment," he said, when he was sure that she was not going to volunteer any information, "we are limited in our choices. The worlds between here and—how do you say it? Delan? Are limited. And, perhaps, we are afraid. Perhaps we seek the advice and the support of the only other intelligent race we have encountered. Although some of our systems are now unsuited for life, we, the Artonuee and Men, face the same threat. Should we not compare notes? Should we not work together?"

"You give us little choice," Miaree said. "The fleet signals."

"Please understand," he said, looking into her eyes. "Our people are dying. Radiations are sweeping many of our worlds. On the rims of the galaxies two great globular clusters are already exchanging sheets of solar flame among their outer members. When the critical moment is reached, and our science is not capable of producing an exact prediction, the worlds of Men will flame and smoke and die."

"It is God's will," Miaree said, for lack of anything else.

"It is an accident of the universe," Rei said, with some force.

The floater was some distance from the rocks. One crag protruded from the water, an offshore upthrusting. Miaree spoke quietly to the younger male crewman. He produced a small, hand-held weapon. There was a flash and the rocky crag glowed, fused, melted with hissing steam into the water.

Rei controlled his impulse to start. He looked thoughtfully back at the steaming water. Then he looked at Miaree, his face grave.

"The decision is made?" he asked.

"We Artonuee are a carefully molded society. We have learned from the ages of our existence that order, peace, planned progress are necessary. Our life form is delicately balanced by the forces of natural evolution. As it is, it is stable, but we know from past disasters of our fragility, of the tenuous hold we have on life."

"You have five planets," Rei said.

"To each a purpose," Miaree said. "Each carefully balanced and a part of the whole."

Rei was silent. The floater, the hum of the drive sucked behind them by the wind, seemed to move on nothingness, rocked slightly by the running waves which sent spray from the prow. He was impressed by the beautiful female's poise, as he had been impressed by the demonstration of the hand weapon. The weapon, he reasoned, was light, a tight beam. The principle was not unfamiliar to him. Each of the approaching star ships, with its precious cargo, was armed with weapons based on the same physical principle. Each ship was capable of destroying anything in its path. Had there been time, for example, he could have burned his way through the asteroid belt which killed his own ship.

When the distant shore was close enough for him to see with his naked eye the forms of other Artonuee waiting at the dock, he spoke again. "Has the decision been made?"

She was not ready to answer, but his directness demanded it. She looked back at the high cliffs and sighed. "We have made no decisions."

"You have five worlds," Rei said. "Each is thinly populated."

"Please," Miaree said. "Not here."

He glanced at the two male crewmen. Sullen faces returned his look. The male eyes were smaller, but of the same general construction. Only the outer circle of facets were missing.

Forbidden to talk, he observed. The female sat with a straight back, her face in profile to him. The air was cool and pleasant on his face. He contented himself with watching the activity on the shore, seeing adult females herd scampering young ahead of them as if to prevent contact with the alien. When the floater drew abreast of the dock there were only two females and a contingent of males on the structure.

Miaree stood, motioned him to precede her. He climbed out of the floater and extended both his hands toward the assembled group. The males stared at him dourly. The tallest of the two females smiled and imitated his motion, both delicate hands extended.

Miaree did not speak. She indicated the passage leading from the dock into a gleaming structure. The doors leading off the passageway were closed. Behind them he heard the musical voices of the young. From the front, as he boarded a ground vehicle, he could see the vast extent of the complex of buildings on the shore of the inland sea. He seated himself in the rear next to Miaree.

The roller moved smoothly over the terrain. There were no roads. However, the ground showed indications of former passage of vehicles and, rounding a hill, he saw something which sent a shock of disbelief through him. It was a primitive rocket. Flared tubes indicated that it was chemical. It was an anachronistic monster in gleaming metals, totally out of keeping with his preconceived ideas about a race which sent messages to the stars. He said nothing, however, since his escort seemed disinclined to talk. He climbed the series of steps to the entrance port, entered, saw the passenger compartment and was taken back in time. Vehicles such as this were rare at home, to be seen only in the best museums which housed the antiquities of his race.

He was alone with the female. He heard the rumble of the engines, felt the lift. He felt a bit like biting his fingernails, but forced himself to be calm until the bellowing of the engines had reached a peak and they had muted themselves. It took long minutes. Afloat in space, he asked, "Chemical fuels?"

She looked at him. Her lips were closed in a tight line.

"Our engines are powered by fusion," he said.

"Yes," she said, in his language.

He spoke in technical terms. He was no atomic expert, but he had passed a basic course before joining the fleet.

"Your faster-than-light ships operate on the same principle, I assume?" he asked.

"Of course," she said.

He did not smile, although he'd thrown into his discourse on engines some hopelessly muddled gobble de gook. Obviously, the female had either been ordered not to share knowledge, or—as it seemed likely from the primitive rocket, which was now approaching an artificial satellite—these lovely Artonuee knew nothing about atomics, were not in deep space, but were limited to chemical travel between their rather closely situated worlds.

He turned his attentions to the docking and was pleased with its smoothness. At least they knew what they were doing with the old fire-burners.

The satellite itself was well-built, had, surprisingly, artificial gravity. This was inconsistent. If they could produce a gravity, why couldn't they find a more efficient means of lifting from a planet?

"Come, please," Miaree said, leading the way from the rocket.

Curious bystanders, mostly males, watched them as she led the way past shops and quarters buildings to the flyer docks. There, on the satellite of The World, the flyer facilities were few, largely emergency repair facilities. There was no regular traffic to The World-gate, but if a lady were in trouble she could come in for first aid to a reluctant convertor. There was only one flyer at the dock. *Rim Star.*

"We could have gone by driver," Miaree said, as she opened the entrance hatch and motioned Rei in. "But drivers are slow and I abhor them."

His interest soared. He noted that the second seat within the small ship seemed to be jury-rigged, set back at an angle behind the pilot's seat. He took his place and Miaree sat in front of him. He looked past her shoulder. The instruments were unfamiliar to him. The ship was too small for atomics. He guessed that the dials measured some electromagnetic force. He watched and listened with great interest as she moved her hands, activating machinery within the hull, sending a crawl of some force over his skin to leave chill bumps there. She spoke into an instrument with her musical, birdlike voice, was answered. The check-out was businesslike. The girl knew what she was about. And then, with clankings and jerkings, they were lifted, pushed, expelled. The full force of the sun came into the front viewer and he yelled in pain, his eyes unprotected. With impressive speed, she closed the viewer, hooding it to expel rays which were harmful to his eyes.

"Sorry," she said.

"You can take that stuff?" he asked. He'd closed his eyes before damage was done, but there were sunghosts dancing there.

He'd missed the unfolding of the wings. They billowed out in an impressive array, thin, almost invisible through the darkened viewer. Looking back, the satellite was already lost in the distance. This thing, he thought, really moves.

She was busy for a few moments, then, with a nod of her graceful head, she turned to him, loosing her belts. "It will not be a long flight," she said. "But perhaps we can use the time to some advantage." Her lips were held in, her eyes darkening in her intensity of manner. "You asked if there had been a decision. I said there had not been. That was only partially true. Whatever decision is made will, in the main, be dependent on what I can learn from you."

"We come in peace," he said.

"But you come."

"The fleet carries only a few," he said.

"May I ask how many is a few?"

"Ten thousand," he said, waiting for her reaction. "They are mainly technicians, but they have brought their families. It was felt that if, working together, we"—he used her term for it—"Delanians and you Artonuee could not find some solution to our problem, then our race could at least survive here among you."

Her yellow hair framed her eyes, which had gone deep purple.

"And in a hundred years," she asked, "how many will your ten thousand be then?" She turned, checked instruments. Flying down the solar wind, the *Rim Star* had reached maximum speed.

"Surely you can share a world with us," he said. "In the name of common humanity."

"And if we say no?"

"I can only hope that you won't," he said.

"But?" She was looking at him, her eyes dark.

"We must survive," he said.

And Miaree shuddered inwardly. His race knew the power source of a sun. The application of such force for purposes of destruction was not an impossible concept. Had not the Artonuee exterminated a life form on The World to protect their eggs? That very subject had been discussed in her last meeting with Mother Aglee. The Artonuee had not used force against any life form in the past few thousand years.

"But," asked Lady Jonea, "if we were faced with a choice between extermination of our own life form and the destruction of another, would we hesitate?"

"We have no weapons," Miaree said.

"We have tools," Mother Aglee said. "Consider the destructive force of the mining torch applied to a life form."

And so it was that Miaree had taken to The World with her a hand-held mining torch. So it was that she had ordered a crewman to demonstrate the tool's capabilities. But in all of the Artonuee worlds there were only a few such tools. And fewer men who knew how to operate them. What weapons had this alien at his disposal?

It had been decided that she should run a strong bluff. As she watched the disc of New World expand, she looked to it. "Should we so choose," she said carefully, "we could destroy your fleet in space, before it reaches the orbit of Five."

Actually, the mining torch had no such capability. It was a tool, not a weapon. It was designed for close-up work on the rocks of the asteroid belt and in the tunnels which bored into the earth.

Rei's estimate of the technological abilities of the Artonuee was confused. First a chemical rocket, then a vehicle which flew, apparently, on the solar wind, a vehicle which hummed with a power unknown to him. It was just possible that they had such weapons. He would, he decided, withhold his threats. He would walk softly and learn.

"We do not," Miaree said, "wish to do so, of course, but we are faced with a difficult decision. As I have told you, our worlds are a part of a whole. Each has its place in the scheme of things. You saw vast, empty space on The World. Yet that space is not a luxury, but a necessity. Our ifflings require huge amounts of food, and they eat only the juplee leaf. You may think, perhaps, that a colony of Delanians on The World would be acceptable? Not so. There is delicate balance. And, such an event would strike straight to the heart of our beliefs, for it is a religious experience when an Artonuee goes home."

"I am not familiar with your terms," Rei said.

Miaree sighed. "I'm sorry. You must understand, then, why we have decided that a long and private series of talks is desirable before we discuss the disposal of your people? Before we can talk rationally, we must know each other. We must know our mutual problems. For example, we Artonuee have long since conquered disease, but suppose your people bring in new strains from Delan? Suppose you yourself have contaminated The World, the heart of our life?"

"I agree that we must talk," Rei said. "That was the purpose of sending our ship ahead of the fleet. We were to make known our peaceful intentions, trade technical knowledge. It was our hope that your own space explorations had discovered habitable planets toward the far rim. If not, we had hoped that we could combine our resources in such a search. For, as you must know, the worlds of the Artonuee will be bathed in deadly radiations when the giant globular clusters reach a critical mass."

She looked at him swiftly, swirls of red in the deep purple of her eyes.

"You don't know?" he asked.

"The Fires of God are still distant," she said.

"Miaree, I must tell you. We, being closer, having observed the collision for a millennium, know the forces involved. To date, the collisions have been minor, and yet you can see them in the night sky. In each of the globular clusters there are a million stars, huge, hot, young, fully fueled stars. It is not a matter, when stars collide, of simple one-plus-one equals-two. The increase is geometric. Our astrophysicists estimate that the final explosion will make two thirds of the galaxy uninhabitable."

"Our scientists see no such immediate danger," Miaree said, hiding her shock, her doubt.

"Then you must take me to them," he said. "I can understand, now, your reluctance to welcome us. Your scientists must know that the end will come, but they are figuring the approach of the fires at a constant speed, right? They have no conception of the multiplication of effect?"

"For that," she said pointedly, "we have only your word. And you have something to gain."

"But I can prove it, with data, with the results of our observations. My god, haven't you sent ships toward the collisions to measure?"

She turned away. He knew, then.

"You don't have star travel," he said.

She looked at him. "Now do you see why we must talk first?"

He shrugged. "So we are further advanced in one

field than you. You have your own advances. This ship, for example. It operates on a principle which is unknown to me. But our weapons are similar. That is, the weapon which you so pointedly demonstrated to me is similar to the weapons of our own fleet. Yet we work for the same thing, for survival of our races. Can't you see that we have that, at least, in common?"

"We have that in common," she agreed. "We will talk of it."

"I am willing to talk," he said. "I will be eager to meet your scientists, to compare notes. I will be more than pleased to send the greeting of our people to your Interplanetary Council, to your leaders. I will open my heart to convince them of our good intentions."

"First," Miaree said, "you must convince me."

He touched her hand. She withdrew it quickly, but the touch, to him, was pleasant. He had been wanting to touch her, to see if she were as soft as she looked. Her fine fur was a tactile pleasure on his fingers.

"Miaree, am I to understand that you are not taking me to the seat of your government?"

"We are going," she said, "to Outworld, where we will have guarded privacy for our talks."

He accepted it. He smiled. "I could not ask for a more beautiful companion. And I pray that there is time."

13

She had visited Outworld as a student. She was familiar with Outworld Gate, a clean, modern facility which was the pride of Artonuee technology. Outgate differed from the satellites of the other planets to an astounding degree. Outgate was sheer luxury. Nothing had been spared in its building, for through Outgate passed the most meaningful beings in Artonuee society, the egg-carrying females bound for their tryst with nature, and a chosen male. Leaving Outgate were the products of a planet devoted to beauty. Outworld diamond sculptors, for example, sent their creations through Outgate to grace the dwellings of the scientists and workers on New World, to lighten the darkness and chill of Five.

Outgate had been seeded with the profuse botanical wonders of the four worlds. It bloomed. It sent a fragrance of flowers into the nostrils of the visitor when the hatch opened and gave vivid promise of the beauty lying below on the garden planet.

The commercial docks of Outgate were lighted around the clock and heavy, utilitarian drivers had right of way approaching the satellite. Monitoring the traffic, Miaree heard departure instructions for a driver of the Fashion Guild, a ship laden with the soft, clinging cloaks and the other garments which were so beloved of the Artonuee female; she heard the arrival of a cargo driver from the belt, its cargo jewels destined for the workshops of the stone craftsmen.

Rei was much impressed by the density of the traffic and admired Miaree's skill in holding the flyer off Outgate until, after a lengthy wait, she was given permission to approach. Ahead of them and behind them flyers drifted, guidance jets being activated to leave a mist in space for a moment before the vacuum ate it.

The flyer docks were crowded, bustling with arrivals and departures. Females with the exciting aroma of pleele passed them as Miaree and Rei stood, watching the dock boys secure *Rim Star* in her berth, and Miaree's heart sank, for the smell, the joyous, expectant look on the faces of her sisters, reminded her of her loss.

Four members of the guard converged on them, voicing their greetings to Miaree, bowing respectfully. Their drop to planetside interrupted the busy schedule of Outgate, for no other passengers were allowed. They had an entire shuttle to themselves, with only the four guardsmen for company.

And so, Miaree came back to Outworld.

Leaving the terminal, they passed a driver being loaded with light paintings, visible in their transparent crates. Rei, astounded, paused. The guardsmen shuffled uncertainly. Miaree, lost in her misery, stood impatiently as the alien examined the glowing, ever-changing works of art. The air of Outworld was sweet to her. There was the buzz of insects and the song of the small, flying creatures and the feeling of peace. She had sacrificed all of it for what? For him? For the alien who stood, eyes wide, watching the workmen load the light paintings?

She moved a few paces ahead, looked out beyond the bounds of the terminal to the countryside. She must stop thinking thus, she told herself. It was past. Her time would come again, when all this was settled. And then out of her would flow life, the glowing, ruby globes of life in the form of fertilized eggs. Out of her they would flow and they would be carefully tested and the accepted ones would be crated lovingly and flown to the old home planet, there to hatch and join the billions of ifflings as they waited for a homecoming. She would then have made her contribution to the continuity of life. Small copies of her consciousness would be crawling the limbs of the huge trees, eating endlessly of the juicy leaves, waiting, waiting, waiting.

She remembered old Beafly, the mechanic, and wondered if his desire had been fulfilled. Had his iffling been female, producing a wingling, as he'd wished? And what would be the fate of her ifflings? Would they produce dull males or flashing beauty in the form of winglings?

As she dreamed, she felt a familiar stirring. "Ah, no," she said aloud. "No, no, no."

They had warned her. "There is always the possibility, my dear," said the doctor who had taken her eggs unripened from her body, "that certain side effects will be manifest. False readiness occurs in about one out of five such cases. It usually is triggered by an emotional experience, simulates the real thing to an amazing degree. Should this happen, there are drugs. Of course, there is a very real desire to mate. But such a mating is a sterile, joyless event. It is to be avoided."

Drugs. Yes. She would seek a doctor.

But the twinge of almost joyful pain in her was gone and the alien was walking toward her, his mouth moving in the barbaric sounds of the Delanians. She put her fear, her doubt, behind her, smiled formally, and motioned the alien toward the waiting roller.

The driver had his instructions. He was silent, glancing with interest at the purple-clad lady and the strange creature who was so like him and yet so different. His instructions did not include an explanation. His was not to question.

The route led them through dense forests, past secluded love nests and artistically designed dwellings, shops, studios. Flowers perfumed the way. Once, Miaree saw a lady and her chosen walking hand in hand along a by-path, and there was once again a twinge of sadness in her.

She diverted her mind by explaining Outworld to the alien. She pointed out the juplee trees from the World; the pleele, native to Outworld; the strange, mosslike growths from Five. She talked of the flying creatures and the insects and explained that all of Outworld was a storage house for the life forms, bird, insect and plant, from the entire system. She explained the technique of light painting and talked of jewel sculpture and, as they passed a settlement of musicians, tried to explain the twenty-tone scale used in Artonuee music. He was baffled as she illustrated by singing the scale, for the upper reaches of the scale were beyond his range of hearing.

He in turn hummed a Delanian air which, to her ears, was strange and rather beautiful, in spite of its simplicity.

They crossed a great river, the roller floating on its huge wheels. Plains of flowers stretched before them, and there, on a hilltop in the midst of the Great Bloom, was the dwelling assigned to them.

The roller stopped before the entrance and the guardsmen, who had followed in a larger vehicle, took their posts as Miaree led the alien into the dwelling.

She greeted the male domestic staff and had one of the males show the alien to his room. In her own room, she freshened herself, changed from the official purple to a sheer gown which let the colors of her body show through, accepted a tray from a domestic, and ate lightly, forcing herself to take nourishment, for she was not hungry. Finished, she inspected the conference room, large, airy. From the front viewer she could look over the Great Bloom. Far away, almost swallowed by distance, a couple ran through the flowers, halted, merged into one, then parted. She felt a joyous leaping in her lower abdomen, smiled, then frowned. The feeling was short-lived. She started to summon a domestic, to send him for the drugs, but the feeling was gone and, hopefully, would not come back. She promised herself to control her emotions. That was all it was, just the emotional experience of coming to Outworld so soon after . . .

She busied herself in preparation for the first conference. When the instruments, carefully concealed, were ready, she called a domestic. "You may escort the—" She almost said *alien.* "You may escort our guest to join me."

Seated opposite her, looking at her across the large, lovingly polished table, Rei saw the change in her eyes. They went from blue to dark as he looked and her face was serious.

"We will begin," she said, "with your telling me, in as much detail as you can, the history of your people, the life style, the philosophies, the dreams, the achievements, anything which comes into your mind."

His first words chilled her. "There are thirty billion of us," he said. "We live on twelve planets of seven closely grouped stars."

Thirty billion. Why, they must breed like the insect of the flower fields.

"We trace our history back over a millennium," he continued. "We have been in deep space for a hundred thousand years. It was made possible by the invention of the hydrogen engine. Star travel was long in coming to us, and it came when the race was overflowing the planets of our original system. Our planners were not as wise as yours, apparently, for we had no system of birth control, and it was a race to determine whether or not we reached the stars or bred ourselves into extinction. Fortunately, the drive was perfected and we spread to the near stars, relieving our population problems. We knew, of course, of the dangers of the collisions. We viewed them, then, as a future problem. Then a multiple collision near our parent system showed us the effect of star union. We lost over two million dead. We had been searching the near stars for habitable planets. It seemed, as we looked, sending ships out into the emptiness, that some benevolent god had created us in the midst of plenty, for our systems were the only habitable systems in a radius of many light years. And, try as we might, we could not improve the drive, which has limitations, to the point of making it possible to explore the entire galaxy, much less leave the galaxy for a universe where the collisions would be left far behind. We had new hope when we received the messages from your people. We were not alone. Perhaps you had answers. But when it was determined that your messages were sent at mere light speed, we questioned the value of them and came to your system only as a last resort."

His words were recorded. His face was captured on film. He talked easily, changing his position in the chair only occasionally, his eyes sincere, looking mostly into Miaree's colorful orbs. And from generalities, he moved into specifics, talking about the Delanian way of life. Miaree got a picture of a network of worlds connected by the faster-than-light drivers, busy worlds, thickly populated worlds devoted to commerce and industry and expansion. The Delanians, she felt, made the Artonuee seem dilettante. Artonuee history, it was true, did not go back a million years, but in a hundred thousand years the Delanians had colonized the planets of seven stars. She felt weak and helpless before him. Her people could not possibly stand before a determined onslaught of even one minor extension of such a power, the approaching fleet of Delanian ships.

She slept fitfully, woke with a curious taste in her mouth. The sweetness of pleele. Dawn was red outside. She stood before an open viewer and stretched her wings. When they folded, they formed the love circle around her shapely rear. Alarm spread through her as her body sent waves of yearning. She shook her head and walked, straight-backed, into the shower, cooling her body with the perfumed water. Fur wet, she stood before a mirror and looked at herself. There was a look about her. A look which she knew.

As the first full day of talks continued, she began to form a picture of the Delanians. It was a portrait in mixed shock and admiration. The Delanian society was full of contrasts.

"We have our poor," Rei said. And she had to search, then ask, for a meaning for the word. It was inconceivable to her to think of people going hungry in the midst of plenty. On the Artonuee worlds, all peoples shared in the bounty of the good planets. Idleness was unknown to the Artonuee. There was no such thing as an unproductive Artonuee. Even severely handicapped persons found a niche in life, gave their share toward the well-ordered continuity of Artonuee society.

Then, while reviewing more Delanian history, Rei talked of the Great War. Again, Miaree had to search out meaning. And there was a wave of sickness in her when she grasped the concept of war. At that moment, she was almost ready to call a halt to the talks, to message the Mother to start the research people to working around the clock to improve the mining torch, to produce weapons capable of blasting the Delanian fleet out of existence before such animals could enter the peaceful Artonuee system. And as she choked back her dismay, Rei continued. The war had devastated three planets, leaving the Delanian society in shock, setting back space exploration for decades.

"We decided then," Rei concluded, "that man would never kill man again. And in fifty thousand years there has been no war."

In present times, the entire Delanian industrial system was working full scale to construct star ships. Before the end came, a percentage, a disastrously low percentage, of the population would be in space.

The idea of vast workshops clanking, pressing, erecting the impressive Delanian drivers took Miaree's mind off the horror of the war and caused a flicker of admiration. She listened. She questioned. She ended the day with mixed emotions. On the one hand, she deplored the Delanians. But she had to be impressed with their racial drive. They were, after all, a race which had sought the far stars. Now, in all their billions, they faced extinction. The concept was too vast to grasp.

Alone in her room, she sought relaxation with jenk. She was feeling the exhilarating lift of the liquor when she joined Rei for the evening meal. They ate in courteous silence, then sat on the outside deck, watching the Great Bloom fade in twilight, silent as the Fires of God rose and gleamed and towered in the sky.

"We have talked little of you, and your people," Rei said.

She talked. Relaxed, sipping jenk, her guest also partaking of the liquor, she spoke mostly of Outworld, her voice low and musical. She told of the great poets who had lived on Outworld, spoke samples of their works. At her orders, the domestics played music tapes. She mentioned that Outworld was the planet of love, and Rei asked for explanation. That led to an extended conversation regarding the life cycle of the Artonuee, from egg to adult.

Rei talked of his experience with the two ifflings. Miaree listened with great interest, for that was an experience which she would face, in time. And no Artonuee had been able to talk with personal knowledge of the feelings one has when an iffling is celebrating its chance at sentient life. She was much impressed to learn that Rei had seemed to receive some form of thought from the ifflings.

"It is strange," Rei said. "You feel such a tenderness for them, while I feel only dread and revulsion. I can still see those terrible maws, so powerful that they cut through the material of my space suit to clamp onto my flesh."

"When two races meet, there is much strangeness," Miaree said, rather defensively. "We find it difficult to accept your method of bearing young. Only our extinct animals bore live young on The World."

But both spoke of the distasteful things with great respect, with a measure of acceptance. A brief session of technical talk, during the day, had impressed Rei with Miaree's power of understanding. She displayed quick comprehension of atomic theory, exchanged some information on electromagnetic wave theory which explained, in part, the motive power of the flyer which had brought them to Outworld. The talks had done one thing. They had convinced each participant that the other was to be respected. Rei had wanted to delve further into the technology of the convertors which powered the flyers. But Miaree cut the technical talk short, to get back to gathering information about Delanian society.

Now it was evening. A soft breeze cooled them. Jenk liquor relaxed them. The scent of the ever-blooming flowers drifted on the wind. The night sky was a thing of awesome beauty. Miaree fell silent, thinking, as she looked at the alien, about his explanation of the breeding process of the Delanians. It seemed to be a cold, sterile relationship. Mates were chosen by vast computers which looked down to the lowest level of the reproductive system to match genes, to refine the race, as Rei put it, to promote racial excellence. The selected breeding pair produced an allowed number of offspring, usually two. The relationship for breeding was often brief, lasting just long enough to fertilize the female. However, in some cases a permanent relationship was formed.

She was favorably impressed when Rei explained that the two sexes were equal in all ways. The idea of male dominance was a false one, she was told. In fact, the crew of the ill-fated star ship on which Rei had come to the Artonuee system had been integrated. Pleasure relationships were permitted.

This concept shocked her, too. Couples did not merge for pleasure, although there was joy in the fertilization process. But for simple self-gratification? Unthinkable. Artonuee females ripened on a cycle which varied, but which usually produced eggs once every five years. Then, and only then, did an Artonuee female seek a male.

Thinking in a spirit of scientific inquiry only, she decided to question Rei further. "You mentioned the female Juanna. Was she your pleasure companion aboard the driver?"

"We were very close," Rei said.

"And did you produce offspring?"

"No. My children were not yet allotted," Rei said.

"I don't understand the pleasure relationship," Miaree said.

"I can see why. Your methods are so much more efficient." He chuckled. "If we were constructed as you are, we would be in the far galaxies by now."

"Explain?"

"A joke," he said. "Our wise men often say that we are too involved in, ah, pleasure. They say we spend too much time enjoying our, shall I say, biological differences. They say if we'd applied the same amount of energy to research, our advances would have been much greater."

"This pleasure relationship," Miaree asked. "How does it differ from the actual mating?"

"In results only," Rei answered. "The male is chemically treated so that there is no fertilization of the female."

She looked at him wonderingly. "The process is the same?"

"Exactly."

"Could you explain, in detail, how the merging is accomplished?"

He laughed. "The male genitalia hardens and is inserted into the female genitalia."

"So. It is thus in our race." She mused. "In fact, as I studied pictures of you without clothing I noted that your male genitalia is very similar to the organs of our males, although differently placed."

"I would be interested in knowing something of your reproductive process," Rei said.

"It is quite different," she said. "First there is the ritual of courtship. The male fondles the female to excite her."

"I left out that detail," Rei said. "It is thus with us."

"Is there attraction, then, between a Delanian female and her mate?"

"We call it love," Rei said.

"An interesting word."

"An interesting process," Rei said.

"And the physical merging," Miaree went on. "How is it accomplished? I mean, where are the female genitalia located in your females?"

"In the vee between the legs," Rei said.

"Strange." Miaree rose. Without speaking, she slipped out of her gown, stood before Rei naked, wings unfolding. She turned. Her rear was exposed by the unfolding of her wings. Her body, graceful, slim, was a rainbow display of colors as she said, "The Artonuee female's reproductive organs are located with an opening at the lower rear. Do you see?"

"Yes," Rei said. He swallowed. And an entertaining thought came to him. Astoundingly, the opening to Miaree's lower body was strikingly similar to the sex organ of the females of his race. He did not know about depth, but in size he knew that their organs would be compatible.

"You are very beautiful, you know," he said.

"Thank you." She shrugged into her gown, covering her wings.

"In size and shape I think that we could blend."

"There would be no fertilization," she said matter-of-factly. "Although in the future I'm sure that we will experiment with artificial fertilization. There is certain evidence, from your encounter with the ifflings, that the life force is similar in our races. It would be most interesting to see what would happen should an Artonuee egg be exposed to the seed of a Delanian male."

"Most interesting," Rei mused.

And so the differences and the similarities were discovered, expounded upon, and digested. For three more days they talked. And the evenings were quiet, relaxed.

In her daily progress reports, Miaree became more and more optimistic. She left nothing out, reporting the Great War as an indication of the danger, but moderating the fact with information regarding the great vitality of the Delanians. She reported in full on their anatomy discussion and received a request from a medical doctor in Government Quad for more information regarding the physical make-up of the alien. At the start of their morning conference she said, "I have a request for physical measurements. Would you please remove your clothing?"

He grinned, rose, and dropped the loose-fitting Artonuee robe with which he had been provided. Miaree, tape measure in hand, measured chest, head, neck, stomach, biceps, thighs. She lifted his limp sexual organ and measured it. He watched musingly.

"It hardens?" she asked.

"Yes."

"What stimulus would be required?" She was smiling up at him. "The medical people specifically requested the hardened measurements."

Rei laughed. Her hand was cupping the organ. "Just a bit more of that," he said.

She looked at him quizzically. "Only this?"

The organ grew. Dutifully, she measured it. "Ah," she said. "Only slightly larger than the average male organ of our people."

Rei was laughing uncontrollably. He sat down weakly and looked at her.

"I fail to see the reason for mirth," she said, frowning.

That night he dreamed of her.

And that night, she had a severe attack of the ripeness.

And on the following evening, they blended.

There was no religious taboo against it. There were religious taboos against many things, but not against blending during a period of false ripeness. It wasn't that it was taboo, it was just that it wasn't done. The Artonuee female wasn't constructed that way. True, there was great joy in the act of fertilization, but it was not for the joy that the act was performed. And there was little data on mergings which happened during false ripeness, for the unfertilized removal of eggs was a medical rarity. There was a certain sterility about the act. There was no possibility of fertilization, so the act was useless, a waste of time. However, she told herself, it was an experiment in racial compatibility, and as such, worthwhile.

The muscles in Miaree's lower abdomen were long, smooth muscles which, in addition to encasing the digestive tract, formed a circle of very articulate tissue centering on her reproductive canal. In ripeness, the lower muscles were extremely active. Made lubricious by glandular secretions, the muscles moved when stimulated by contact with the male genitalia, simulating the rolling of continuous bands of softness which, during fertilization, moved the male organ ever deeper into the cavity. To Rei, who was not unaccustomed to sexual acts, the effect was miraculous. And the flexibility of the ripe, distended, rounded, lovely bottom of the Artonuee female allowed for approach from both front and rear. In the frontal position, lips pressed on lips, the female's soft, erotically muscled rear twisted forward between her slim legs. From the rear, the softness pressed upward, engulfing all of Rei's sexual apparatus.

But how had it happened?

It began with a discussion of poetry. "Poetry is beauty, and thus you are poetry," Rei said.

"There is a certain impreciseness of meaning in your language," Miaree said, watching the Fires in the dome, sipping jenk, fighting the ripe, full feeling, trying to drown, in jenk, the urge to run into the Great Bloom to find her chosen.

"You are poetry and can be translated," he said. "Would you like a demonstration?"

"By all means," she said.

"This is you," he said, lifting from his set of notes a duppaper sheet, hand-inscribed.

> Your lips are caramel, my dear
> Full, mellow, sweet, deep gossamer
> A myriad thing
> A plural one
> A juplee ripening in the sun.
>
> Your eyes are innocent and low
> As arc burned briefly holds its glow
> And lashes sing
> And brows two plus
> Make triad tongue, gratuitous.
>
> You are, my dear, a lovely theme
> Artonuee music, endless dream
> Of light and sound
> And blended reeds
> And ripened scent of pleele seeds.
>
> Part of a whole, yet idioblast
> Descended from a wholesome past
> Of strength to hope
> And sense to fear
> The march of doom across our sphere.
>
> But smiles, my dear? You have a few
> Each look distinct, vermillion hue
> They bridge the gap
> And draw us close
> And that is when I love you most.

"It has a certain rhythm," Miaree said.

"When a lady has a poem written about her, the poet expects more than cold analysis," Rei smiled.

"The lady is appreciative," Miaree said. Her eyes were light blue. Her smile was genuine. But had he noted the aroma of pleele about her? Had she told the alien that such an aroma had a significance? She couldn't remember. Yet it was strange that he would speak of the scent of pleele.

She had been remiss in her duty. A simple order. A dosage of a prescribed drug. She had been warned. One out of five experienced the false ripeness, and ripeness, the most emotional experience an Artonuee female could have, deadened the brain, left it floating in the soft sea of desire.

"Would you walk?" she asked. He arose. As they descended the stairs he put his hand on her arm. Her soft fur was sweet to his touch, and his touch sent cascades of fire leaping through her veins. "Please," she said, pushing his hand away.

For the touch was an important part of the ritual, the ritual she'd missed, the pleasure of which she'd been robbed by duty.

And the Great Bloom was fragrant in her nose, soft under her bare feet. Her gown flowed. Her wings strained to be free, to show the glowing colors of ripeness. Well, she thought, why not? The alien did not know the symbolic meaning of freed wings. It was dark. The domestic staff was in quarters. No one would see. She loosed her gown, let the wings flow, flexing them.

"Lovely," Rei said. "Why do you ever cover them?"

"Tradition," she said.

"A foolish tradition, to hide such beauty."

She walked ahead, realizing, as she did, that her wings were forming the curl of invitation at their lower extremities. But again, it would have no meaning for the alien. Only an Artonuee male would know, and there were no males about.

Head up, eyes measuring the evil gleam of the Fires, she ran lightly ahead, wanting to be alone. Her foot, as she ran, sought the earth, found only a slight drop as she ran over a depression, went down, down. She tumbled into the flowers and lay there, momentarily breathless. She felt strong arms lift her, heard his voice.

"Are you all right?"

His hands were heated as she sensed them through her sheer gown. His arms were powerful. His body and his breath warmed her. A vast, all-devouring weakness surged through her, and she opened her lips, keened a love song. It was eerily beautiful. It silenced him. He knew it wasn't pain she sang, but he did not know the full meaning, save that it sent a wave of emotion through him.

"You're not hurt?" he asked.

"No, no," she breathed, her lips parting, extending.

"What is it? What's wrong?"

In answer she lifted her head, cradled as she was in his arms. Her long, sensitive lips touched. She keened through them, the beautiful love sound. And as he kissed her, her wings fluttered wildly, wildly, and her hand touched him, ran under his robe to press against his warm skin.

He carried her to the dwelling. Her lips continued to seek his, her mind overpowered, her body in command. Ripeness sent its sweet smell into the warm, night air.

"Thus, and thus," she instructed him, in the darkness of her room. His hand following her hints, caressing, feeling the smoothness of her fur. "And thus," she whispered as, naked, she knew the joy of merge.

14

And so, my young friends, we have been introduced, through the conversations of Rei and Miaree, to the Delanian society. Discussion, please. Alaxender?

All the data is not in, sir. However, I see the Delanian society as being much like ours. It is based on trade and commerce among scattered worlds. The colonialization of distant star systems has been made possible through the development of a faster-than-light drive of some sort, although the Delanian star ships seem to be more severely limited in their range. I would suspect that the use of a fusion engine indicates that the Delanians did not possess anything similar to the blink drive. If they were using anything similar to the blink principle, such vast amounts of power would not be necessary. I would guess that the Delanians approached the problem by the application of brute force. There is a formula—

Yes, Alaxender, we know your Trojan genius for mathematics.

Brifley, sir, although small multiples of light speed are possible through the application of force, if one considers the Auguste Loophole, the results tend to diminish to the point of no return when the speed nears three parsecs per year. Giving the Delanians, then, a speed of light times ten, that would place the Delanian systems about thirty light years away from the Artonuee. If I am right in assuming that the translation equates all time and all figures and measurements to our standards, it took Rei three years to reach the Artonuee system. The fleet was about a year behind Rei's scout ship. I would assume the Artonuee galaxy to be roughly the same size as our own, about eighty thousand light years in diameter, so that places both of the civilized systems in one small sector of the galaxy, likely in one spiral arm.

Yes. Your point, Alaxender?

Sorry, sir; I was rambling, wasn't I? I was merely trying, in my mind, to get the picture. We know now that there is a more imminent danger than expected by Artonuee scientists, that the collisions are expected to become more intense and to produce some sort of a multiplying effect. However, the explosion of a super nova moves through space at less than light speed. I fail to see how the Artonuee system is endangered, at least immediately. Rei speaks of two giant globular clusters in collision. Incidentally, this is quite a thought. We know the power of a super nova. It is difficult to imagine the simultaneous explosion of a million suns, but it happened, as witness the time-lapse film which we have all seen. But sir, assuming that this collision, which we have recorded, is the one which caused Rei to fear the destruction of all the inhabited areas of his galaxy, how long would it take the explosion to reach the Artonuee system? If the exploding material expanded at light speed, it would be thirty plus years. Since such material travels at considerably less than light speed, there was no need for panic, because the Artonuee worlds would have been safe for a hundred, perhaps even two hundred years.

Comment, Elizabeth?

I think Alaxender is forgetting that the Artonuee are a very old race, with a different sense of time. They have a written history which goes back further than our own. To them, with their over-all sense of history and destiny, two hundred years would seem but a moment.

Well taken, Elizabeth. Yes, Julius?

The Delanian system is much nearer the point of collision, and their sense of doom must be much more acute than that of even the Artonuee. I am surprised at Rei's patience during the long talk session with Miaree. If I had been in his place, I would have been screaming and yelling. I'd have said, "Look, you dumb bitch"—pardon me—"you dumb female, my people are going to die."

Yes, Alaxender?

Sir, I have calculated the total energy necessary to be a threat to the Artonuee worlds from the given distance. It is in the order of 3×6^6 solar masses of hydrogen.

Ah.

My point, sir. I think Rei, for some reason, is lying.

Ah?

Oh, no.

Leslie.

He wasn't lying. Perhaps he was unduly alarmed. But he was so very, very sincere in his relationship with Miaree. I think it's just beautiful the way they fell in love.

You are not the first, Leslie. Stella?

I think Rei's seduction of Miaree was a superb example of chauvinism and I agree with Alaxender. Rei is up to something.

3×10^6 solar masses of hydrogen, sir, is about equal to a small galaxy.

Alaxender, perhaps you would like to propose this problem to your astrophysics class. Let us confine ourselves to the analysis of Delanian society and the implications of the facts brought forth in the preceding section of the fable. John?

It wasn't a bad poem, sir. And I was astounded by the very pleasing naiveté displayed by Miaree. She reminds me of a sweet, innocent child. I think it is rather touching that these two, one far from home, his friends dead, the other a victim of a personal tragedy of deep meaning to her, should find pleasure in each other.

Elana?

I think the seduction scene reveals something of Rei's character. Miaree is merely a victim of her biological urge. But Rei has real freedom of choice, and he chooses to seduce her. Put my vote with Alaxender and Stella's. Rei is up to something. I have the impression that Rei's society swings free and easy where sex is concerned. While we know that Artonuee youngsters are placed with what they call a Chosen Mother, thus getting some form of family life, we have no clue so far as to the disposition of the Delanians' carefully programmed children. It has been demonstrated throughout our history that the family unit is beneficial. I suspect any society which ignores the family-unit concept.

Do we condemn Miaree for her actions? Martha?

Negative, sir. Although she finds it necessary, probably after the fact, to rationalize her actions, she is, as Elana said, a victim of her biology. Further, there are no taboos against sex for the sake of mere pleasure in the Artonuee society, so she is treading new ground. Although she did not have complete freedom of choice in the first instance, in later instances—

Let us not get ahead of our reading. Clear Thought?

For good or ill, Rei has, I think, convinced Miaree of the good intentions of the Delanians.

Excuse me. LaConius. Sleep does not come easy to you in the comfort of your bed?

Sorry, sir. Just resting my eyes. You were asking?

Just for a comment, LaConius. If you can keep your eyes open that long.

Sir, you mentioned it yourself. The wormfly of Omaha III.

I did, some twenty-four hours past.

Let's consider the wormfly, sir. It was beautiful. It was deadly. It was prolific. To irradiate an entire planet was impossible. Insecticides also destroyed the beneficial insects imported to pollinate the crops. To control the wormfly, the farmers of Omaha III bred a huge number of sterile male wormflies and released them.

Since the female wormfly mated only once before death, a mating with a sterile male prevented a hatch of wormfly larvae. The fly was exterminated within a few years.

Ah. Have you been reading ahead, then, LaConius?

Ah, no sir. I haven't. I'm doing a term paper for astrophysics on the Q.S.S. phenomenon, and there is so much intriguing material that I haven't had time to do more than read the assigned material for this class, sir. Incidentally, I'd like to thank you for putting me onto the subject of my paper with your mention of the Q.S.S.'s.

My pleasure. But if you have not read ahead, LaConius, you are very perceptive. Has the thought occurred to anyone else that the mating of Rei and Miaree could have more than personal consequence? Ah, Martha, you have read the entire legend? Good. Tomorrow, you may begin our class reading, since you are so familiar with the material.

15

The eggs were the color of dead flesh.

Paying tribute to age-old feelings, she had fashioned a nest of silken bed coverings. The process was painless and somewhat erotic.

But there was no joy.

A living egg was, to all females, a thing of beauty. Glowing, a living egg seemed to pulse with life, emanating that most odd and lovely ruby radiance, the ancient, all-sacred color.

Although she had known what to expect—she was not the first—she could not control the tears which flowed from her disturbed deep purple, faceted eyes. The color of dead flesh. Inert. Lifeless.

She left them in the silken nest as she cleansed herself. Aside from a pulsing weakness in her lower rear, she was normal. She stood, wings furled, beside the bed. She had known what to expect. She lidded her eyes, pushing away the tears, bent, scooped the dead eggs into her hands, and walked slowly to the disposer. Then within seconds it was over.

Outside, a world was in the process of change. As she listened to the hum of the disposer, she could hear, above the soft, final sound, the rumble of industry, the movement of vehicles, the low roar of an engine under test.

She told herself that she was very young, that there would be time.

Her eyes changed, became intense blue. A look of determination firmed her lips. She donned gown and cloak. In the style of the new female, her wings were freed, gleaming with the ever-present colors of happiness. Outside, the weather of the narrow equatorial temperate zone was at its best, the sun, although distant, warm and cheerful. There was a briskness in the moderate temperature, the hint of cold from the frozen poles. The horizon was near, surprisingly near. It was a small world. And it was throbbing with vitality.

16

Bertt, designer and builder of the finest flyers, was an unhappy man. Not content with changing his world—a world which he had chosen for its remoteness, for its limitless spaces—they were now changing his life and, indeed, his very way of thinking. Although Bertt was not an introspective man—*male* (he corrected his use of the alien term)—this was perhaps the most disturbing thing of all; to have the thought patterns of a lifetime shattered so casually.

Surely, he thought, God would move. Surely, even a God who had in the recent past shown little interest in the Artonuee, leaving them to the doom signaled by the Fires, would be too proud to see her daughters flaunting themselves, wings unfurled and displayed outside their cloaks, simpering and fawning over and being pawed by the muscular Delanians. Had the entire race gone mad? Did thousands of years of tradition and common sense have so little value?

But it was not only the shamelessness of the new breed of Artonuee females which upset Bertt. He had not been able to get away from his shop, to go roving, solitary and in communication with his God, for months. And the last time he had ventured up into the Big Cold he had been forced to detour away from one of his favorite routes, bumping and sliding over unexplored ice fields, because of the presence of one of the several industrial plants which were springing up from the wild regions of his world like noxious metal growths.

It was his clean air which was being spoiled by the refuse of the huge, clanking plants, by the exhausts of the heavy traffic in drivers. And the temperate zone was becoming impossible. Hastily erected dwellings in multiple units were taking all available land areas, denuding the virgin growth of stunted trees. They were even building into the shallow waters of the equatorial sea, hiding its blue waters beneath metal platforms, defiling even the depths in their efforts to gather more raw materials for the building of still more plants and still more dwellings and administration buildings. Now there was talk of melting the northern ice cap to uncover more usable land.

As a member of the Council of Five, Bertt had protested mightily. Melting the ice cap, he said, would submerge the tiny amount of temperate land at the equator. No, they told him—the Lady Miaree speaking for the slick-faced aliens—the surplus water would be evaporated and pumped into space. The ladies in Nirrar, he was to discover, while exposing their wings in invitations to the aliens, had decided that this world, his Five, was expendable. His planet, his chosen home, that once empty, beautiful, inhospitable but glorious world, was to be gutted.

"We must stand," he told his fellow male members of the Council of Five (Five was primarily a male world). "We might fight them."

They reacted as frightened walklings. They stuttered and vacillated and wavered and backed down. And his world was changed, almost overnight it seemed, although it had only been four years since the fleet landed on the frozen wastes and disgorged thousands of aliens, men, women and children.

Still, it was impossible not to be impressed by the purpose. He was firmly convinced that it was against God's will, but nevertheless, the idea was inspiring. And already the fabric of his religion had been ripped by the mere revelation that the aliens could, with their awesome power sources, prove that God's Constant was not sacred. And it was exhilarating, in a way, to work with the aliens. He prided himself on being able to grasp immediately the complicated process of their power source, and he was more than equal to them in other fields. Even the most brilliant among them had difficulty in connecting the loose principles which went into the fashioning of a mires expander; but to give credit where credit was due—he was a fair man—once grasped, the principles swirled around in the alien brain and came out with twists which, once expounded, seemed so elementary that he was ashamed of not having thought of them himself.

Yes, there were compensations. He himself had flown. He, Bertt, the builder, had been forced to admit that he was wrong and he, being the male that he was and prideful of it, admitted that he was wrong. Perhaps newness was not all that undesirable when it produced a machine like the *Rim Star II.*

Aboard that small vessel, he, along with the man called Rei and the Lady Miaree, had vaulted further from the home worlds than any Artonuee male. And now the combination of convertors, expanders, and power which had made the *Rim Star II* blast effortlessly into deep space, eating distance at a God-defying rate, was being developed to power vast star ships, the size of which dwarfed anything ever dreamed. And that—that vast, unbelievable project—was only the beginning.

In spite of his misgivings and his sadness at seeing his world changed, Bertt could not conceal his eagerness. He considered the nights to be wasted, slept only the minimum number of hours, was at his shop before the Fires cooled in the warmth of the distant sun. More often than not he found Untell there ahead of him.

She was there, alien woman, hair chopped carelessly close to her scalp, fleshy body bent over a work bench, on a morning in the beginning of the year, probing into the intricacies of a mires expander, her eyes reddened by sleeplessness. She had been his work mate for four years, and his revulsion toward her largeness, her alien fleshiness, had gradually changed, first into a grudging admission that the alien had a brain, and then into an admiration which, as the months passed, wiped from his mind all his conscious awareness of their differences. Together, they were changing more than a world.

"You have not slept," he said.

"Didn't want to lose it," she said, not looking up. "I think we can test as soon as I ..." She applied a cold torch, fused tiny contact points.

"The new circuit was satisfactory?" Bertt asked, pushing his arms into his working garment and leaning down, head close to Untell's.

"Perfect," she said.

"Resistance readings?" he asked, watching her fingers move with a nimbleness which he envied.

She chuckled. "As predicted."

He breathed deeply and allowed himself a smile. He had mistrusted his own figures.

His momentary irritation at finding Untell still in the shop faded before his interest, for if he were right—and it was his theory, developed after having his mind opened through contact with the almost heretical courage and intellectual curiosity of the alien woman—he, Bertt, would have a place in the combined history of the Artonuee and Delanian races. If he were right, he, Bertt, the builder, would also bring further curses down on his head from the priests, for his discovery, if it tested, would open new avenues of thinking which would relegate the vengeful God of the Artonuee to a position even more inferior than She now held.

But Bertt was not thinking of God as he busied himself. He was thinking of the fantastic force held there, within the altered mires expander, in two tiny bits of red-brown metal machined to be exactly a 0.1-inch cube.

Untell assisted as he made the last connections, his

blunt fingers less nimble, but sure. Then they stood before the assembled expander and the alien smiled and shrugged.

Permission for the test had already been granted by the Lady Miaree, Overlady of Five. The drone driver was fueled and waiting, an obsolete vehicle not deemed worthy of conversion to the new power source. All test units within the driver had been tested and checked repeatedly by assistants.

Bertt summoned a young male, a bright lad fresh from his Chosen Mother, supervised the careful placement of the expander onto a small roller, rode the roller, with Untell by his side, to the launch pad. It took just thirty minutes to install the expander. It took just under four hours to run a last-minute check on all systems, then, protected behind a thick viewer, they watched the drone fire, lift, and disappear.

When the drone, moving at driver speed and thus taking long, long hours (during which Untell napped and Bertt paced nervously) reached empty space beyond the orbit of Five, he ordered an assistant to report readiness to the Lady Miaree, who had expressed a desire to witness the test. When she arrived, robed in purple, comely beyond his belief, accompanied by the alien, Rei, he nodded to Untell, awake, tense, seated at the main console.

A signal lifted from the surface of Five, flashed through empty space, activated a trigger mechanism on the drone. The altered circuits on and in the mires expander reacted instantly, and briefly measured, a force of six hundred trillion tons—blasting from Bertt's 0.1-inch cube of metal of atomic weight 63.54—was met by equal force coming from the electrons in an exactly similar cube at the other end of the complicated mires circuit.

It happened so tremendously fast that only instruments could measure.

To the viewers, it seemed that the drone merely disappeared, but during a disheartening post-mortem, the

instruments showed a tiny increase in the drone velocity which, upon examination, put the fire back into
Bertt's eyes. The force of the electrons had not, as it
seemed, merely ripped apart all the atoms in their immediate vicinity. No. For a millisecond, that incredible
force had been channeled. For one tiny moment Bertt's
theory had worked.

Seeing the telltale figures, he looked up at Untell.
His face, which had been downcast, brightened. She
nodded, understanding.

But the Overlady had questions.

"My Lady," Bertt said, "you can see. For an instant
we had it. For a measurable instant we were in control
of a force which staggers the imagination."

"Dear Bertt," the Overlady said. He lowered his
eyes. He did not like the use of terms of affection. That
was a Delanian characteristic, and unbecoming in an
Artonuee. "When you approached me on this subject,
telling me of the possibilities, I warned you then that
we have no time for pure research. We have present
capability to fulfill our plans. We must concentrate on
the known. Your services are badly needed. The services of the worthy Untell have been sorely missed.
How much longer can we spare you?"

"A month, Lady. Give us another month. We are so
very near." He bowed respectfully.

"No longer, Bertt. In one month the engines will be
ready for installation in the first of the giant star ships.
In two months, another fleet arrives, and your knowledge will be much in demand as we share our progress
with the newly arrived scientists."

"Yes, Lady," Bertt said, shifting impatiently. Red
tape, he was thinking. Bureaucratic thinking. He
longed for the peace and quiet of his world as it had
been before the arrival of the aliens, altered that to
wish for unlimited time and the help of his new friend,
Untell. Give them a month, a year, and they would
beat God, the bureaucrats, and space itself.

17

Evening. A swollen, yellow sun half-high. Five's South Cold. Desolate. Beautiful. Humidity in the air tinged golden yellow, bursting, flaring, raying the sun's light into streaks of red-gold fire and shadows on the ice ranging from black to purple and, far away, his movement. He was one of a restless breed. But, oh, Lady Mother, God of Artonuee, he was beautiful.

Lost from view behind an ice upthrusting. A hint of the cold loss of sadness in her until he reappeared, nearing.

Bundled into cold-wear, he appeared to be a furry beast picking his way across the eternal ice, and try as she might, she could not bring her eyes to lower, to study the urgent reports lying on her knees. She was desolated without him. The basic chemistry of her blood cried out for him.

"Lady," she mused aloud, "you are in a position of responsibility." Thus driven, she picked up the first report.

At New Nirrar, on the western equatorial land mass, a clash between two groups of females. Words. Reliable witnesses reported that the Delanian women had first resorted to violence. However, one witness, a reliable Artonuee male, said that the violence was the result of dire provocation on the part of the Artonuee females, who taunted the Delanians as animals of the ancient

116

past, bringing their young into the world bloody and wet with vile body juices.

The Artonuee male, one Bruun, technician, said in his statement: "Seeing that an incident was brewing I, as a responsible adult male, tried to avert unpleasantness. Speaking only logic—" How very malelike, Miaree thought, "I tried to dissuade the emotional women and females from further insults and was rewarded by being called a rather derogatory Delanian name, a name with which we males have become familiar through the discourtesy of the aliens, a name I choose not to repeat."

For the record, the investigating official had inserted an explanation. Bruun, the technician, was called a cannibal, referring, of course, to the instinctive behavior of the Artonuee walkling in consuming the iffling-preserved flesh of a homecomer.

"At this juncture," Bruun continued, "one of the females rose unnecessarily to my defense, saying words to the effect that I, Bruun, was a respected member of the Artonuee community and not subject to ridicule by creatures who carried their young living in their bellies. Before I could speak, blows were exchanged."

Angrily, Miaree tossed the report aside.

Rei was near. She rose, waved. She keened the love greeting and received, in answer, a loud shout. Then he became interested in a curious ice formation, and she, with a sigh, picked up the discarded report. The females involved were wing-flaunters, of course. She used the term in her mind without censure, for her own wings were outside her cloak.

She dictated recommendations. Extra work tours for the Artonuee females. Punishment to be deemed just for the Delanians by the Delanian local Board of Control.

Next, a request from Plant Seven for a rush allotment of diamond drills.

For the first time in years she remembered her rock, the rock she'd discovered in the asteroid belt so long,

long ago. She chastised herself for forgetfulness, for diamonds were in great demand, made a mental note to check her old flight log for the coordinates of the asteroid and to send a driver, priority class, to mine the jewels.

It was amusing, in a way. Once the diamond asteroid had meant only more flight time to her. Now it could aid in the greatest undertaking ever conceived by the best minds of two great races.

A progress report on installation of engines in the first giant star ship, revolutionary engines, engines which were a direct result of her alliance with Rei, the Delanian.

But, Mother God, she was tired. She lidded her eyes. Her head rested on the velvety cushion of her chair and she allowed herself the luxury of pure idleness. Musing, she remembered Rei's excitement.

She was taken back, in memory, to Outworld. The first days. The golden flush of joy at their first merge. The splendor of love. Love. A word which was now as much Artonuee as Delanian. Love. A sweet sound on the lips. A touch. The electric stir of fur to the touch of a skinned hand, a hand so strong, so tender. Then, time had no meaning. Then, before the arrival of the first fleet and the nervous confrontation of two separate races, it was only Rei and Miaree and the flood of well-being which his kiss engendered in her and the pleasure of shared knowledge and intimacies and endless days of talk as they sat, or lay, or walked in the Bloom and then, with Mother Aglee becoming querulous in demanding a report, the lovely flight from Outworld to New World and the pride she felt in Rei when he mastered the techniques of flying so easily. It was then, during the long, upwind flight, that he discovered the possibilities. As Miaree and Rei merged into one, so the technology of the two races merged and brought forth not dead-flesh eggs, but a triumph of engineering. For the mires expander and the convertors, lowering, as they did, the mass of the flyer, eliminating inertia, fitted with the fusion engine of the Delanians as Rei fitted with Miaree.

When she explained, he fell into deep thought, and suddenly, ignoring the view of New World ahead, he was busily scratching figures and formulas and trying to explain to her that with nearly zero mass a ship could be pushed to twice the current speeds of the Delanian drivers. Moreover, the limitations on the size of a star ship were completely removed. With the new system, a ship could be built as large as technology allowed, as big as a planet.

Changes. Vast upheavals in thought, in the Artonuee way of life. The area of space which could be explored was suddenly doubled. A single technological breakthrough, a single instance of cooperation between races, and a civilization groaned and, in spite of the obstructions of the priests, began a change which would affect every individual on four worlds.

There were times, during the hectic course of a day, when she wished for the old, peaceful times when God was God and the Fires were there, unchanging, eternal, approaching with deadly slowness. She had almost shared the fears of the priests when, with near-silent and awesome power, the fleet landed on the hastily prepared pads on the out planet, cold Five. They were many in their thousands, and all were powerful. The women, although considered beautiful, were oversized, fleshy. They worked alongside the men in an impressive display of vitality to build dwellings.

It was she who took the problem of combining the flyer with a Delanian engine. Appointed by Mother Aglee as Overlady of Five, charged with coordinating the peaceful integration of the aliens into the life of the planet, she sought out Bertt, explained all to him, asked respectfully for his assistance. To expedite the trial of a new ship, she submitted *Rim Star* to alterations and, crowded into the small space inside the year, saw the distortions of faster-than-light speed, pushed the tiny ship to light times twenty and looked at the home worlds from a distance which reduced the sun to a tiny, insignificant star lost in the vastness of the galaxy.

She remembered the near revolt of the priest-led males when it was announced that the Delanian fleet was only the first of many to leave the constellation of Delan at one-year intervals. She remembered the all-night sessions of the Council, the heated discussions among the inner circle, the final decision, hastened by astronomical observations of the collisions which confirmed Rei's warning of impending disaster.

And she remembered how Mother Aglee had wept while announcing the decision.

"This," Mother Aglee had said—and five years later Miaree remembered every word—"is a time of crisis. It is a time for difficult, sometimes terrible decisions. Our talks with the Delanian authorities are now concluded, and to reassure my people, let me say that the Delanians are aware of and have empathy for our peculiar and necessary arrangements of life on our habitable worlds. The sacred groves of The World will not be disturbed by alien tread. The ordered life of New World will not be shattered by uncontrolled settlement of aliens. The beauty of Outworld will be held inviolate.

"Yet, since our races face a common danger, we must not turn our backs on fellow sentient beings. We must make a place for the Delanians in our society, thus enabling us to work together with them against our common doom. It has been decided to allow the Delanian fleet to land on Five. There, on that cold and inhospitable planet, we will begin our work together.

"It has been said that Five will be changed. I cannot deny this fact. And Five is an Artonuee world, thinly populated though it may be, cold and desolate though it may be. Let those who cry out sacrilege and bewail the coming of the Delanians remember that, save by a quirk of God or nature, it could be Artonuee fleeing from the Fires of God, seeking haven. And let us remember that the Delanians come in peace, seeking only our friendship, our help, our cooperation in working together to escape the destruction of our worlds.

"I am able to tell you, at this time, that two of our fellows, a Delanian and an Artonuee, working together as we must work together, have made possible a dream. It is obvious to all that the Delanians have mastered star travel. Yet they are limited, to a degree, by God's Constant. This mutual discovery by members of two cooperating races has, in effect, doubled the range and the speed of the Delanian light ships. Let us remember, as we hope the Delanians will remember, that it was Artonuee technology, combined with their own, which made such a giant leap forward possible."

Changes. Necessary changes. In order to produce synthetic foods, the Delanians needed certain raw materials. A portion of the Artonuee fleet of drivers was required, while plans were being drawn for the construction of new drivers, new factories. Artonuee scientists were at first uprooted from their dwellings near the Research Quad and flown to Five to consult with the Delanians. Then, with an absence of equipment on the cold planet, with the meeting of the two races proceeding smoothly, Delanians were allowed on New World to work in the Quad with their Artonuee counterparts. Delanian botanists were escorted to Outworld. After an angry meeting of the Council, a Delanian scientist was given permission to study the feeding habits of the ifflings on The World. The Council of Five appointed two Delanian representatives. The two races worked together in harmony, coming closer, ever closer, but not without clashes. When the second Delanian fleet, carrying twenty thousand male workers, arrived on Five, crowds of alarmed Artonuee males paraded past Government Quad. But the decision had been made. The twenty thousand workers were welcomed, for the drain on Artonuee manpower was severe, the demand for raw materials ever increasing as work proceeded on the building of the first huge star ships. The colony of Delanians on New World numbered over two thousand after the arrival of the second fleet, doubled with the arrival from deep space of the third fleet in the third year following Rei's arrival. Three thousand Delanian men on New World began to contribute to the most profound change in Artonuee life.

It was a change with which Miaree was familiar, for she had been the first to experience it. The wonder of it never left her, was with her, full force, as from the viewer-enclosed snugness of her South Cold weekend retreat on Five, she watched Rei bend and examine an ice formation. It was a basic chemical change in her body, a change which altered a thousand centuries of evolution. It was a simple, unpredictable change involving the interaction of Delanian sperm with the reproductive organs of the Artonuee female. Simply put, the alkaline seminal fluid of Rei reacted with female hormones to cause a slight irritation of inner tissue. The irritation was identical, in all respects save one, with the natural change which indicated the formation of eggs in the female body. The effect was to induce an artificial state of ripeness in the Artonuee female which had all of the emotional force of the actual thing. Once injected with Delanian seminal fluid, an Artonuee female walked in a constant aroma of pleele and experienced, with her lover, all the joys of merge.

The cyclical mating urge of the Artonuee female, all-powerful, was now a permanent part of Miaree's life. And looking at Rei's powerful back as he bent, she would not change it, would not trade it for the most perfect of ruby eggs. And her discovery of bliss was shared by others, many others, more and more as the number of Delanian males increased in the system. The love of a female for her man was a heady, irresistible drug. It was an obsession which could be mastered temporarily, to allow a female to function in society, as long as her lover was near, as long as the night could be filled with that most lovely of experiences, love. And if the price to be paid came in the shape of a sacred egg the color of dead flesh, there were billions of ifflings, and it had been proven that abstinence lessened the irritation, allowed the female to function as nature had intended.

In a time of racial excitement, of new and rewarding experiences, of hope, of a lessening of respect for the discredited Artonuee God, there was a future. For the first time since Artonuee astronomers had understood the meaning of the Fires of God, the race could look forward to something other than eventual extinction. There was a vast storage world of life, teeming with ifflings. The flow of winglings and walklings did not lessen. The decrease in the number of ifflings was insignificant. The stars called. The greatest building program in the history of the race was underway, centered on Five, an Artonuee world already transformed beyond recognition. Destiny called, and destiny, for multiple numbers of Artonuee females, involved that new and exciting word, love. Alliances were made and sundered. Since neither race had evolved into permanent relationships between the sexes, the alliances were often multiple. No Delanian man was deprived of the beauty of the Artonuee females. Even Mother Aglee took a Delanian lover, and keened sweetly of his love.

The elected leader of four populated worlds appeared at functions of state with her colorful wings exposed.

And gradually, Artonuee men accepted the change. They too found compensation. It began with the workers on Five. Stimulated constantly by the pleele aroma exuded by artificially ripe females, they found that the Delanian women were not resentful of their men's attention to the Artonuee females. In fact, the alien women found the males of Artonuee to be fair and took them to bed and suffered none of the chemical changes which altered the Artonuee female.

The first Delanian child to be born on Five arrived days after the landing of the fleet. At first, in the confusion, there were no reliable records of Delanian population increase. When a census was taken some three years later, it was discovered that the birth rate of the Delanian women was 1.2 children every two years. Yet the numbers were relatively small. It was only with the arrival of the fourth fleet, with entire families, that the Interplanetary Council recognized the problem and issued a request that Delanians control their population at zero growth. The request was promptly acknowledged and accepted. A potential crisis was averted. The good intentions of the aliens were reaffirmed.

"Ah, love, love," she keened, as Rei entered. She met him with open arms, felt the strength of his body. His lips fired her heart. The long night was ahead, the urgent reports forgotten, put aside for the morrow. In his arms she was not Overlady of Five. She was simply female, and loved.

In his arms no fears were allowed, doubts were banished. Gentle, loving, true, giving his love only to her, he was incapable of hurt. She would trust him with her life. And because he was a representative of his race, all of his race was good.

One day she would deprive herself of his love long enough to produce her contribution of ruby eggs. One day. Meantime, the work load was frightful and the nights were too short and she was merely a female, loved and loving and thankful to her God for her good fortune.

18

Assembled in space, it stretched over five miles in length. Square angles allowed utilization of all areas. Connected sections contributed to the length, but were removable. Huge enough to transport a section of juplee forest, powerful enough to push past the side portal of God's Constant, it gleamed in the harsh, un-filtered sun, absorbed the blackness of space on the out-sun side. It was ready.

In *Rim Star II* she floated near, saw the towering walls of the ship extend above her. Skillfully she circled it, admired it, measured it with her eyes. Pride pound-ed in her breast. She put her hand on Rei's and smiled. He understood.

"Yes," he said. "The first. The first of many."

Monitoring the communications frequencies, she knew it was time. She withdrew to a safe distance. Searing light flared from the trailing engine compart-ments. Aboard, outsized convertors hummed. The movement was slow and majestic at first; then, with an acceleration which left her breathless, the star ship dwindled to nothingness. She followed it on her instru-ments, saw it. As it hit the side portal of the Constant, it disappeared.

Three years in the future, it would be back. It would carry a host of workers, workers sorely needed to mine the asteroid belt, to continue the gutting of hot First Planet for its metals and materials, to dig into the center of Five, to man the assembly lines and operate the mining drivers and labor at the thousand-and-one tasks ahead during the construction of a fleet of like ships which would release millions of Delanians and Artonuee from certain death before the Fires brought their doom. And while in the Delanian systems, it would serve as a prototype for a million of its kind. The entire resources of thirty billion Delanians would be diverted into building the star ships. The vast fleet would sweep outward, following the lead of scout ships which, at that very moment, were searching the stars toward the opposite end of the Galaxy for habitable planets. Planets would be found. Planets would be settled. Together, Artonuee and Delanian would spread across the empty reaches, planet to planet, system to system, taking with them their life, their technology. Doom would be thwarted. Life would go on. And in the end, the labors of such as Bertt and Untell would allow an escape from the doomed galaxies, would allow life to be eternal in safe, green worlds of promise far from the Fires.

Meanwhile, there was endless work and continual problems and Rei's love to inspire her. A day seemed endless, yet the days became weeks and the weeks years, and the first star ship returned to disgorge eager workers and the dread information—information which traveled at light speed and thus had not reached the Artonuee system—that the collision of the two globular clusters just outside the spiral arm had begun. Death raced toward the Delanian worlds. There, a crash program of building was underway, which, by the time the star ship reached Five at light times twenty, produced thousands of ships. The first of the final wave would be arriving in less than a year's time.

The knowledge stunned Miaree. Somewhere there, where her eye could not see, billions of beings were to die. And she was helpless to prevent it. She wept for them, Rei's strong arms comforting her. And she worked harder than she had thought possible, for the

Artonuee, luckier than the Delanians, had been given time. The first waves of radiation and fire would strike the outlying Delanian worlds in less than three years. Artonuee would have a minimum of twenty times that time span in which to prepare to evacuate the system. Although she wept for the Delanians, she rejoiced for the Artonuee. In sixty years she could build enough star ships to save all, to forest a ship with juplee and select prime ifflings for the long trek to safer planets. She could build a ship designed to salvage the artistic beauty of Outworld—flora, fauna, artifacts, art works. God was good. God had forgiven.

Thankful that she was young and able to cope with the long hours, she was everywhere. Inspired by Rei's presence at her side, she was capable of going thirty-six hours without sleep. Her mind, expanded by the learned knowledge of Rei's people, could absorb the most difficult of technical problems.

Miaree was forty, just at the end of her young adulthood, when Mother Aglee kissed her lover one final time and boarded a ship for the last flight. With the office of the Mother vacant, the five worlds of the Artonuee throbbing with frenzied activity, Miaree agreed to allow powerful members of the Interplanetary Council to advance her name for election. Because of her travels and her prominence in the building program, she won easily.

Only ten days after Mother Aglee sought her iffling, Mother Miaree, wearing the robes of the first lady of all the Artonuee, entered a large conference room to be briefed on the state of the system. She had been so involved in the administration of the factory planet, Five, that she had not been able to keep abreast of problems outside her own field. The sobering facts which were thrust upon her from first one serious-faced official and then another left her in a state of shock and sorrow.

Spant, Delanian, Co-administrator of Space Exploration: "Lady, more than two thousand Light Twenty Scouts are in the outer stars. Although good news could be reported at any time, the results to date are discouragingly negative. As you know, the formation of planets is a rarity, requiring such a combination of conditions as to make only one star out of a half-million a planet producer. Aside from two planets in the early stages of producing water, no habitable worlds have been discovered. I request the authorization for the construction of an additional five hundred scouts."

Rei, by appointment of the Mother, Supervisor of Raw Materials: "Lady, time is too short. We must consider the exploration program a failure in its present form and adopt Contingency Plan Two."

Mother Miaree: "For those of you who are not briefed on Contingency Plan Two, it is simply this. Should the exploration program fail, as it has failed to this date, at the time of final decision, when the exploding stellar material begins to threaten our system, we embark on the fleet of star ships and use the fleet, itself, as an exploration tool. Perhaps a word from Bertt, Star Fleet Overlord."

Bertt, Star Fleet Overlord: "Ladies, males, Delanians. Although passenger space is the primary object in the construction of a star ship, it has long been recognized that long periods of travel could be necessary. We never had any guarantee that good worlds would be discovered within a reasonable distance. Thus, we have constructed each ship to have the capacity to live in space almost indefinitely. Unfortunately, the space required for growing synthetic foods, and for the other life support systems required, cuts down severely on the space to be allotted to passengers. Should disaster strike immediately, we would be able to save only a small percentage of the combined populations of our races. However, it is estimated that we have a minimum of twenty years to complete our building program. Should we make certain technological breakthroughs, the picture could be improved. If we allotted more of our time and our available resources to research—"

Mother Miaree: "Dear Bertt, that is an old argument, one which was settled long ago."

Belle, Overlady of Outworld: "Lady Mother, attention is required to the continued destruction of our most beautiful planet. As you know, the Council opened Outworld to Delanian settlement some ten years past. Since then, the Delanian population has grown out of control with new arrivals. Delanians outnumber Artonuee on Outworld ten to one. Their numbers strain the resources of the planet. We have been forced to utilize for dwellings and industry a large percentage of our natural parklands. Where once the Great Bloom stretched for five hundred miles, unbroken, sprawling cities now soil the air. This desecration—"

Argun, President of the Delanian People in Exile: "Would the lady prefer that two billion Delanians die on the home worlds?"

Mother Miaree: "None of us would wish such a tragedy. Too many Delanians died. Their death saddens all of us."

Caee, Overlady of The World: "Mother, it is true that we are all saddened by the tragedy which has swept the home systems of the Delanians. I deplore before God the sad fact that, together, we were able to save not more than one-fifth of the total population before the Fires destroyed all who were left. It is truly a cosmic tragedy. However, six billion Delanians were saved by the star ships which were built here, by our people and their people, and by the star ships which were built in the Delanian systems. We Artonuee have opened our arms to our Delanian friends. We have welcomed them in their billions to our small worlds, and we have paid a terrible price. I do not deplore the sacrifice of the Artonuee. No. Indeed, we owe a vote of thanks to the Delanians for alerting us to the doom which we had considered to be remote, a happening of the distant future. So our lots are cast together. It is not merely petty thinking, then, when I say that I must insist that action be taken regarding the production of

Delanian children on The World. I do not, of course, have to tell the Mother the grim statistics of iffling mortality—"

Mother Miaree: "Perhaps you do. Remember, I have spent my time on Five and in space."

Caee: "The information is classified."

Mother Miaree: "All here are suited to receive classified information. They would not be here if they were not."

Caee: "Yes, Lady. If you would care to read the last report."

Mother Miaree: "I do, indeed, care to read the last and all reports regarding alterations to The World. I want all material pertaining to tampering with the life cycle on our home planet in my office immediately following this meeting. In the meantime, perhaps you would be so kind as to inform me when it was decided and who decided to allow even one iffling to die."

Caee: "Mother, I am sorry. I thought you had been informed. It was decided by the Interplanetary Council, at the urging of Mother Aglee, to allow iffling reserves to fall to a working one-on-one level some seven years past. At first, this was easily accomplished by the mere non-replenishment of stock as homecomings lowered the iffling population. Thus it was possible to utilize a portion of the juplee forests—"

Mother Miaree: "Am I to understand that the sacred juplee forests have been leveled?"

Caee: "Mother, there are five hundred million Delanians on The World."

Mother Miaree: "God the Mother!"

Argun: "Lady, it was a difficult and terrible decision for your predecessor and for the Council. It was felt—"

Mother Miaree: "Damn you all, tell me. Iffling mortality?"

Caee: "Mortality is at a low level, and selected females are being commissioned to produce fertile eggs to replenish—"

Mother Miaree: "How low is low? What is the state of the iffling population?"

Caee: "Lady, a blight, thought to be the result of atmospheric pollution, has hit the forest. Ifflings are dying at a rate which reduces the population by approximately seven percent a year."

Mother Miaree: "And the growth rate of the Delanians on The World?"

Argun: "In accordance with our agreement, we are holding all Delanians to zero population growth."

Mother Miaree: "As of now, there will be no child births allowed to Delanians on The World."

Rei: "Lady, is this not a harsh decision?"

Mother Miaree: "Dear Rei, I did not assume this office to preside over the death of all the Artonuee. All my life I have faced the fact that, someday, the Fires would end Artonuee life, but I will not accept a slow and lingering withering of our race through the destruction of that which is most sacred to us, our home world. We have sacrificed. Our worlds bulge with six billion Delanians. No. Now it is time to call on the Delanians on The World for a sacrifice on their part. Argun, I respectfully direct you to issue orders preventing any further conception on our home world."

Argun: "It will be done, Lady."

Mother Miaree: "Caee, I want daily reports from you on this situation. I will not be satisfied until there is no iffling mortality. Do you understand? And Belle, I appoint you to personally select females to produce fertilized eggs. You may ask for volunteers. That failing, you have the authority of this office to use any means to insure that the iffling population is maintained at a safe level. If it requires the incarceration of suitable females until their ripeness produces fruit, then consider it an order."

Caee: "Yes, Lady."

Mother Miaree: "For the information of all, a report from the Supervisor of Raw Materials."

Rei: "Lady, before this conference began, Fleet

Overlord Bertt reported to me that construction is at a halt on the three hundred star ships nearing completion, and new starts have been postponed indefinitely. The fact is that we're running out of materials. Although some exploration continues in the asteroid belt, for all practical purposes the belt has been mined empty. Our prime source for the needed metal is now First Planet, and conditions there, so near the sun, are, to say the least, bad. Our engineers are working on methods to mine the sunside of the planet, but such efforts are not expected to produce returns for another five years or more. Meanwhile, the further explorations for metals on Five produce nothing. Five is a gutted planet. The mines of New World, Outworld, and the small area where mining is permitted on The World are spent, produce only low grade ores which do not meet the demand. The star ships drafted into temporary duty as mining ships, traveling to the three arid planets of the star Seberian, require months for a round trip. Nevertheless, they are providing us with our main bulk of useable metals. There is a severe shortage of diamond drills, and I would respectfully request the Mother to issue a statement asking all citizens to make available for industrial use their private jewels."

Mother Miaree: "Noted and done."

Rei: "Although we have not, as yet, experienced food shortages, an agricultural crisis is imminent. Arable land has been used to build factories and dwellings. Ninety-five percent of our basic foodstuff is now being dredged from the seas, and the heavy use of shallow water growth for synthetics threatens to unbalance the growth cycle of the salt water agricultural areas. I would think that consideration of food rationing should be undertaken by the Council during the next session."

Mother Miaree: "I will talk with Council leaders."

Bertt: "Lady Mother. I have watched my chosen world be stripped of its resources and its beauty. Although this saddens me, I do not regret it, for will not my Five be consumed, seared, destroyed, when the

Fires reach us? And is it not true that all our old worlds will meet their ends in the Fires? I agree, of course, that The World must be preserved until the exodus to insure the continuation of our race. However, with a present capacity to move only sixty percent of our combined populations, and the future grim, as far as raw materials are concerned, would it not be wise to lift the exploitation limitations of the two planets which still offer prospects of production? I refer, of course, to New World and Outworld."

Belle, Overlady of Outworld: "Our garden world is already spoiled beyond hope. Would you put mining shafts in the last remaining parklands? Would you ship ore in huge rollers down the streets of our cities?"

Bertt: "Would you have millions burn in the Fires, sitting happily in the last remaining parklands atop the metals which could have saved them?"

Mother Miaree: "Your point is well taken, Bertt, but such decisions are a matter for the Council. If you will prepare your proposals I will present them."

Jenee, Overlady of the City of Nirrar: "Lady, it is a small matter, perhaps, since we are faced with problems of cosmic size, but would you express an opinion on the desirability of posting members of the guard at strategic locations throughout the city? As you may know, the exuberant spirits of the Delanian young sometimes take a destructive course. The problem is not a major one, but their activities have been known to interfere with the administration of the city, which is, as you know, vastly overcrowded. Destruction of property and forced merge are merely two of the symptoms."

Mother Miaree: "Perhaps the President of the Delanians has a comment?"

Argun: "Lady, give me as many guards as you can. I will augment their number with enough Delanians to stop such outrageous activities."

Mother Miaree: "Done, Argun. Thank you for your help. We Artonuee have not faced such problems in the

19

Five's nightside sparkled with the lights of industry. The atmosphere, artificially thickened to produce a greenhouse effect, caused the glow to be diffused, hid the equatorial low lands, behind their huge dikes, under swirls of cloud. Incoming from New World and Mother Miaree's first top-level conference, Bertt swung his flyer into dayside, called Fivegate for landing clearance, and then, waiting, let his eyes feast on the inspiring sight of a million star ships, lined up like great beasts of black space in a holding orbit.

The construction area, just past Fivegate, was visible as he landed. Cargo shuttles crowded the gate, idle. Bertt walked rapidly to the control center. A star ship from the ore planets of Seberian was within communications range. Soon the smelters would glow again and work could continue on the hundreds of ships in various stages of completion.

In spite of the hectic events of the past twenty years, Bertt was still uncomfortable in closed spaces. Although it was gratifying to be able to man a powered flyer, he was not a space nut. And the closed atmosphere of the gate was heavy in his mind. He boarded a shuttle as quickly as possible, and already anticipating a few hours of luxurious freedom from responsibility, began to draw, for perhaps the millionth-plus time, the circuits of a mires expander in his mind.

Once he had seen the release of unbelievable power.

Once, with his Delanian friend, Untell, he had been on the verge of the greatest discovery of all.

Delanian power was an improvement. And the combination of the convertors and the Delanian power had reduced the shuttle ride to planetside to minutes. Great strides had been taken in space travel. Still, the two cooperating races faced an uncertain future of star-roving in that ponderous fleet which was being assembled in orbit around Five.

He was thinking of the prospect of finishing out his allotted time in a closed atmosphere. Huge as the star ships were, he, lover of spaces and the lost solitude of his old world, did not relish the idea of a lifetime of imprisonment in a star ship.

Because of his position and his need for privacy, he had been allowed to keep his old dwelling. It was small, but it sat in the midst of an acre of undisturbed land. And adjoining it was the old workshop where he had designed and built the finest flyers ever to ride the solar winds. He ate the tasteful synthetics, sipped synthetic jenk, dozed in his chair to recover from the shock of planet change, but his mind would not be idle.

The dream was always with him.

They had been so close.

A year and they would have had it. Working with Untell, he, Bertt, would have created a source of power so vast that the universe would have been opened to exploration.

Sighing, he rose and stretched tiredly. He shrugged into a work garment and trudged into the shop. He mused before his bench for long minutes, his eyes following the convolutions of the incredibly complicated circuitry of the altered expander which had once released the energies of the electrons in two tiny cubes of soft metal. Once, twice, three times he had watched with the same results. A significant and measurable channeling of the force and then disintegration.

Where had they gone wrong?

He had traced the theory in its complications thousands of times. He traced it once again. In the mind, on duppaper, it worked. What was the hidden fault?

When his assistant came in search of him next morning, Bertt was discovered sleeping, his head on the workbench. The assistant smiled sadly. The old man was still playing with his toy.

20

Argun, President of the Delanian People in Exile, was a virile man in the prime of his life. Although he carried a heavy responsibility, he lived with an élan that kept his outlook youthful and optimistic. As a youth, he had helped to tame a world which had presented more problems than the little ice ball the Artonuee had loved so much before Delanian vitality had made the place liveable. His genes were the finest, and even before leaving the home worlds, he had been allowed four offspring with four different chosen women. Two of his sons were among those selected to live. And Argun had sired a daughter and a son since coming to the Artonuee system. His seed would be preserved and preserved well. He took great pride in that.

At his headquarters in the Government Quad in Nirrar City, adjacent to the Mother's building, he maintained two Artonuee mistresses and was not averse to spreading that particular form of Delanian joy to others, casual acquaintances longing for a dose of the Delanian drug.

For his personal staff, he had selected the strongest and wisest, both men and women. He was a man with a purpose, and he worked toward that purpose with untiring vigor. He had seen enough death. Those who had not been on the home worlds at the end could not possibly understand.

Seated with Argun was young Rei, who warmed the Mother's bed.

"You have completed the assignment?" Argun asked.

"It is confirmed," Rei said. He sipped the Artonuee liquor, for which he had acquired a taste, while Argun drank heartily from a mug of synthetic Delanian grog.

"Quite a dish, no?" Argun asked.

"She was a good specimen," Rei said.

"Indeed," Argun said. "I know. I envy you the job of knocking her up. Would have done it myself, but I don't want it said that I take undue advantage of my position."

"Your fairness to our people has never been in doubt," Rei said.

"But not the Artonuee, huh?" Argun said, laughing. "My boy, you're too soft."

"I was the first to land on an Artonuee world," Rei said softly. "I have worked closely with them for twenty years. They are an admirable people."

"Ah, that Artonuee cunt," Argun said. "Now *that* is admirable." He drained his mug and set it down with a clank. "But I have six billion people to worry about."

"Sir—"

"Six billion," Argun said. "And I watched twenty-four billion die. I saw it, damn it. I was there. I heard my own son cry when he was told that he had not been selected. I had to deny his last minute plea. I gave the orders which brought instant death to thousands in the port riots. I saw my men turn their weapons on their own people, brothers, sisters, lovers. Have you ever seen flesh after it's hit with a burner? It stinks. It's the color of dirt. And when the ray hits, the flesh crawls and jumps and moves even after the brain is dead. And I had to say, "open fire!" I had to give the order."

"It was a tragedy, sir," Rei said.

"Tragedy? Damn, man, it was horror. Can you comprehend the death of twenty-four billion people? No one can. It staggers the imagination. We can understand the death of a man, or a few men. You helped in the post-mortem of the first expedition, didn't you? I thought so. You saw the way the limbs were torn from bodies. Did it affect you?"

"It affected me," Rei said.

"Think of two billion more bodies. Think of them dying slowly from radiation and then being seared by flame. Is that a pleasant picture?"

"No, it is not. But neither—"

"There is no alternative," Argun said, standing. "Of course, if you should volunteer to stay—" He grinned as Rei shifted uneasily. "Goodnight, then, my boy. It is not pleasant for any of us. We must do as we think best for all of our people. In the meantime, we drink, no?"

"We drink," Rei said, gulping the jenk.

"And our geneticist wants another chip off the old Rei block," Argun said, showing his teeth suggestively. "Up to another session tonight?"

"I think not, sir."

"Soon, then. She's a knockout. A farm girl from old Tagour. Knockers out to here. Huh?"

"Yes," Rei said. "Soon."

Later, fanned by Miaree's ecstatically fluttering wings, hearing her love keenings, he shut his mind and lost himself in her living, moving softness.

21

You read well, my dear. Thank you. We have covered much ground today, and there is little time. I hope
that all of you have been thinking ahead toward the
paper which I told you I would ask you to write giving
your conclusions and your feelings toward the fable.
Now. In form, the section of the fable we have covered
today is somewhat episodic. By skips and starts, it
covered a period of how many years, Tomax?

Twenty, sir.

Are there any among you who have not been stimulated to the point of being forced to finish the final portion? Ah? Elizabeth? LaConius. But LaConius knows,
eh, LaConius?

Sir?

Elizabeth, no curiosity?

Sir, I was dying to finish it, to find out what happens, but the dorm matron forced me to observe
lights-out, and the charger in my privacy light has
failed, so I could not read under the sheets.

Then we will allow you to read the conclusion tomorrow. Now, in the brief time remaining before we
partake of sautéed olix steak, fresh in from Alaxender's home on Trojan, I would like you to consider this
passage, or this series of excerpts, from a paper done
by our sleepy LaConius. For which, incidentally, he
has earned the honors in this particular project. La-
Conius has handed me the paper, a project undertaken

for his astrophysics class, with a request for proofreading. I fear that our LaConius is a rather atrocious speller. Nonetheless, the paper is of some interest. The subject is the Q.S.S. phenomenon. Q.S.S. or Quasi-stellar Radio Sources, are rather puzzling astronomical objects located—as determined by the calculations of the red shift—some one billion light years away from our galaxy in the general direction of the constellation Cygnus.

But let me quote young LaConius: 'Radio generation in the Q.S.S.'s, broadcast on every frequency known to man, is thought to be the result of acceleration of ultra-high-speed electrons moving in a powerful magnetic field. Although a thorough and lengthy study of the Q.S.S.'s has failed to provide a range of answers, it is believed by authorities in the field that the electrons were freed in some cataclysmic explosion. The release of energy is not a strange happening in a universe built on the explosive energy of the hydrogen atom, but the amount of energy radiating from a Q.S.S. has led astrophysicists to believe that the energy originated from an entirely new type of energy source. The power generated by a typical Q.S.S. is measured in the area of 4×10^{46} ergs per second, or ten times the amount of energy radiated by the largest known galaxy.

'The baffling thing about the Q.S.S. is that a typical diameter measures only fifty light years. When we consider that our own galaxy is eighty thousand light years in diameter, the amount of power emanating from the relatively tiny Q.S.S. becomes even more astounding. Estimating mass from the observed size of a typical Q.S.S., the amount of energy released totals more than the energy in all of the available electrons. If a small galaxy were exploded by thermonuclear processes, the energy released would not equal that of a Q.S.S. Spectrography indicates that the Q.S.S.'s are moving away from our galaxy at a uniform speed. Emission lines in the optical spectrum indicate the presence of hydrogen, magnesium, ionized neon, oxygen, and other gases.'

There is more, but I think that much will give you the idea. Questions? Alaxender?

I can only conclude, sir, that a Q.S.S. cannot possibly exist, and yet it does.

Yes. Ah. The dining hall signals its readiness.

22

Miaree, First Lady of five worlds, had a tendency to calculate time from the arrival of Rei. The calendar systems of both races were bulky and unwieldy, both measuring years, as they did, into six figures, seven in the case of the Delanians. There were shortened forms of writing a date, of course, but it was convenient to think in simple terms. Rei plus twenty. Rei plus twenty-five.

In the year of Rei, twenty-five, the Mother of the Artonuee received a request from an old friend, Bertt the builder, Star Fleet Overlord.

"Feeling the approach of my time," Bertt wrote, "it is with much regret that I request to be relieved of my duties."

Sadly, she sent her permission. "It would be a great honor, my dear Bertt, to have you stay in my dwelling on your way home."

Since the jobs were so interconnected, it seemed logical to appoint her consort Rei to fill Bertt's position. This meant, of course, that they were often apart, and separations were agony for her. It was a time of sacrifice, however, for the distant astronomical observatories in space sent daily reports of the swelling explosions in the constellation of Delan. The Delanian scientists had been accurate to within twenty percent in their predictions of the multiplication effects of the violent coming together of the two giant clusters. Their margin of error

144

was on the conservative side. In the path of the expanding jets of energy, stars, fed by the debris, joined in the paroxysm. The nighttime sky was a thing of harsh and terrible beauty.

These were, then, the last days.

On The World, giant machines burrowed under the deep roots of the juplee trees, lifted tree and earth to waiting cargo drivers. In orbit around the Artonuee home world, a hundred star ships waited, holds prepared, to become the home in space for a virgin forest. The World was being sacked that the Artonuee might live. And as the forests were moved, miners followed, destroying all in their path, for there was no longer need to preserve a world which was facing doom.

For those Artonuee who worked on The World, it was a traumatic experience.

The shortage of raw materials was an ever-present irritation. Rei chafed, shouted at his subordinates, drove the miners who were at last allowed to gut the home world. The twenty-percent error in prediction of the time left meant uncertainty and terror. Even the crash program of utilizing all available materials would fall short.

The drivers which had once worked the asteroid belt, a vast fleet, were being melted down for their metals. Nothing was spared. The Evacuation Committee, headed by Argun, President of the Delanians, was assembling the land and air vehicles necessary to transport the population to the waiting star ships, and all vehicles not needed in that effort were expendable.

In Nirrar, the decorative metal fronts of government buildings were being pulled down. Monuments to past Artonuee greatness toppled from their pedestals and joined private flyers, rollers, all scrap metals in the melting vats.

Food rationing was in effect, for the vast food storehouses of the star ships were being filled. Enumeration of the population was almost complete. Each individual

member of both races carried and guarded his assignment card, for it meant life. On all five of the worlds,
practice evacuations were being carried out to familiar-
ize the people with the methods of loading.

Loading would be a lengthy and complicated process.
Miaree, burdened with the endless details of office
and carrying, along with all her race, the sadness of the
coming departure, left details of that massive operation
to the Evacuation Committee. She was only one female.
She could not attend personally to all details.

She thanked God for the strength and vitality of the
Delanian men, for without them the work would never
have been accomplished. Outnumbering Artonuee
males by almost six to one, they bore the main burden
of labor.

It was not a time for crisis, but then crisis has never
been possessed of a conscience, and when the Delanian
women began their revolt there was nothing to do but
deal with it.

It began on Five. Led by Untell, who had once
worked with the builder Bertt, mobs of women paraded
past government houses demanding change.

Miaree considered the spokeswoman's demands.

"For too long have we, the flower of Delanian wom-
anhood, suffered at the hands of the shameless Artonuee females. Our men, lured into liaison with the
Artonuee, have all but deserted us. We face a long
journey into the unknown, and we refuse to undertake
this journey in the company of Artonuee females who,
because of the peculiarities of their anatomy, are such
attractive temptation for our men. We demand total
segregation of races aboard the star ships."

"A bunch of featherheads," said Argun in conference. "This protest is an isolated event and will pass.
Our races work too well together to allow a few
hotheads to spoil the partnership which has developed."

"They are your women," Miaree said. "I bow to
your knowledge of them."

However, as the situation worsened, she was forced

to reconsider. A half-million Delanian women stormed Government Quad, threw stones through the viewers of the buildings, severely mauled members of the guard.

It was the same on all inhabited planets. Everywhere Delanian women rose up, demanding that the relationship between Artonuee females and Delanians be sundered aboard the star fleet.

"Oh, Darling," Miaree said, in the privacy of her dwelling. "It would mean—"

"They will not force us to part," Rei said.

"But your own president often states that a leader cannot ask something of his people which he himself would not share. How could I tear my sisters from their lovers and, in all conscience, remain with you?"

"There will be a way," Rei said, closing her lips with his.

To placate the Delanian women (whose activities were throwing the overall plan out of balance, delaying the plantings of the juplee trees in their assigned ships, forcing cancellation of practice loadings) the joint governments of the two races announced that racial integrity was to be maintained aboard the fleet.

To give her forlorn sisters hope—for they were, she knew, as devastated as she—the Mother announced, "New worlds will be found. There the two races will live side by side. In times of peace and plenty, the harsh measures required by present-day conditions will doubtless be rescinded."

With Belle, Overlady of Outworld, Miaree considered the problem of space for the treasure stores of Artonuee art.

"Sadly," she told Belle, "we are forced to abandon much. For you see, the building program has been slowed by the lack of materials. The accelerated approach of the Fires has caught us short. I weep to think of the necessity to leave the paintings of Janlee and Peeri. We must pick and choose, dear Belle, and control our emotions, for is not life the important thing?

Would you trade one life, say, for the jewel-sculpture portrait of Lady Andee?"

Her conference with the weeping Belle was shortened by an urgent request from one Runder, assistant to the Overlord of the Fleet, who cited urgency and priority as his reason for demanding time with The Mother.

Runder was a young male in his prime, a male who had adopted the dress fashions of the Delanians. He stood respectfully before Miaree's desk. "Lady," said he, "I am Runder. Before the time of change I worked on Flyer Haven. I had the pleasure of servicing My Lady's personal flyer when she was but a youth."

"You were chosen by old Beafly," Miaree said. "I remember." She smiled. "You tuned *Rim Star* well."

"Lady, I have always done my best. I have been rewarded by being allowed to perform tasks of responsibility and value. There have been no complaints. Thus, I have allowed myself the self-gratification of presuming on the Lady's time to ask why I have been so summarily relieved of my duties. If I have presumed too much, I am sorry."

Miaree frowned. "My dear Runder. This office, I fear, is a demanding one. It does not lessen the importance of the position you have held when I confess that I know nothing of what you state. Could you brief me?"

"Yes, Lady."

"First, please sit."

"Thank you, Lady. I was appointed to my position by Overlord Bertt these six years past. Since Bertt's primary interest was in the star fleet, the responsibility of seeing to the administrative duties of the Overlord's office fell to me. When the honorable Bertt retired to his workshop—"

"Hold, Runder. Would you repeat that?"

"I said, 'When the honorable Bertt retired to his workshop—' "

"It was my understanding that he was preparing for homecoming," Miaree said.

"I am sorry." Runder's face was mobile, showing his sorrow. "I did not intend to violate a confidence."

"Then Bertt is not ready for homecoming?"

"He is well, Lady. I'm sorry that I mentioned it. However, since I have ... He was tired. Since the population of Five is largely Delanian, he asked that I forego my rights of senority and allow the appointment of a Delanian Overlord. I agreed. However, events of the past days—"

"Forgive me, Runder. I am interested in Bertt. It is not like him to forsake his important duties without reason. Your thinking, please."

"Lady, I fear that the pressure has touched Bertt. For years he has pushed himself too hard. No one can say that he did not do his assigned job well. In fact, it is my opinion, enforced by my personal observations, that Bertt should be named a Hero of the Artonuee for his administration of the building of the fleet. However, during the years of crisis, Bertt pursued his dream in addition to doing his tasks. I fear the toll on his health was too great."

"His dream?"

"As I remember, Lady, you were present when Bertt and the Delanian woman Untell conducted tests of an altered mires expander in conjunction with the electron forces of a soft metal."

"Yes."

"He has never abandoned the idea that he could make it work, Lady. He spent many hours, sleepless nights, in his private workshop. He is there now, puttering, sleeping little, working on his hopeless task."

"Poor Bertt." She shook her head sadly. "But Runder, your reason for requesting this appointment, please."

"As I said, Lady, I agreed to allow the appointment of a Delanian Overlord in the dual capacity of Five Overlord and Overlord of the Fleet. I continued to handle the administrative duties of the planet. It was only when I questioned the release of Artonuee males from positions of responsibility in the fleet that a coldness developed between my office and the Delanian Overlord. I received no satisfactory explanation of the dismissals, and when I insisted on an inquiry, I was summarily notified on the stationery of your office, Lady, that my services were no longer required."

"This office?" Miaree inquired.

"Yes, Lady."

"I signed no such order," she said.

Runder was silent.

Miaree placed a graceful finger to her nose, mused. Then, with a decisive movement, she pushed a communicator and asked Rei to come into the office.

As he entered, the load of responsibility seemed to Runder to melt from her lovely face. Her smile was a thing of beauty. "This is the worthy Runder," she said, "Assistant Overlord of the Fleet. He has a legitimate inquiry. It seems that I somehow agreed to release him from his duties without justification."

"Not you, Lady," Rei said, returning her smile. "It was I."

Miaree's brows lifted in question.

Rei turned to Runder. "Your haste in coming to Nirrar prevented you from finding further orders in your slot," he said. "Although I do not remember exactly, I am sure, considering your position of responsibility and your experience, that you are among those who are assigned to supervise the migration of Artonuee from Five."

Runder's brows knit in question. "May I ask, sir, for more details?"

Rei was leafing through a thick process book. "Yes," he said. "Here it is. Runder, Assistant Overlord, transferred to Migration Fleet in the capacity of First Officer."

Miaree, too, was puzzled. However, she kept her silence, knowing that Rei would explain.

"My Lady," Rei said, "this was the subject of the afternoon conference which I had requested. Runder's problem is connected with the recommendation which we were to discuss. Would you care to hear it in brief at this time?" She nodded. "To facilitate the final loading, in accordance with the joint decision to segregate races aboard the fleet, it is advised by fleet officials that all Artonuee first be moved to the home world, leaving New World, Outworld, and Five as assembly points for the loading of Delanians. Thus, all Artonuee will be in that section of the fleet which contains the juplee ships. Artonuee and their juplee ships will be a unit."

"It is logical," Miaree said.

"Since the population of Artonuee is lowest on Five," Rei continued, "it would be best to begin there."

"I agree," Miaree said. "Does this answer your inquiry, Runder?"

The young male bowed. "Yes, Lady."

"The movement of Artonuee from Five to The World will be a dress rehearsal for the final flight," Rei said. "As you examine your orders, Runder, you will see specific requests for detailed reports covering many subjects. Not one of these subjects is unimportant. The information we can gather during this short movement can be extremely valuable when we begin the final movement."

"I understand," Runder said, standing, backing toward the door. "I beg My Lady's forgiveness for intruding."

"It was good to see an old friend," Miaree said. "Please feel free to contact this office at any time."

Alone with Rei, she voiced a bright note of love, smiled. He leaned to touch her lips with his. "Since I'm here," he said, "I should broach another subject which, I have been told, will be brought up this afternoon."

"Oh, Rei, I wish it were over," she said. "I wish it would turn out to be a dream and that I'd awaken with the smell of the Bloom in my nostrils and you beside me, back on Outworld."

"Yes, darling," he said. "But the conference."

"Damn the conference," she said.

"The Evacuation Committee is going to make a recommendation to cut the size of the juplee fleet in half," Rei said.

Jolted back to reality, she stiffened. "That, of course, is impossible," she said.

"Lady, remember that some members of the committee, Argun among them, were on the Delanian worlds at the end. They saw thousands of their brothers burned down when, in panic, they tried to storm the ports in an effort to squeeze aboard the already laden ships. They saw the first of our worlds begin to smoulder, and the smoke of the planets was the death pyre of twenty-four billion Delanians. They are not unjust men, but they question the giving over of so much space to trees and a billion and a half ifflings."

"All this has been explained to them," Miaree said. "The transportation of the ifflings and the source of their food is not open to negotiation."

"I know," Rei said softly. "But I merely wanted you to be prepared."

She was prepared. She delayed her entrance to the conference room until all were present and seated. Then she swept in, robed in official purple. They rose, Artonuee and Delanians, bowed their heads in respect. She motioned them to be seated, waited for the shuffling noises to cease.

"Before we begin," she said, standing regally at the head of the large table, "I will comment on one item which appears on the agenda. I am sure that the concern of our Delanian comrades is genuine and without malice. However, the fact is that we have covered all details of the transportation of our ifflings, and the subject is no longer open for discussion. I will add only this. The best minds of our people have worked for twenty-four years on this problem, and their conclusions cannot be questioned. One hundred star ships are the absolute minimum required to transport the juplee forests. Even with the addition of this one hundred to the number of ships required to transport the entire Artonuee people, the portion of the fleet alloted to the Artonuee is less than one-sixth the size of the entire fleet. Proportionally, according to the relative numbers of our two peoples, we would be entitled to more ships. It is fortunate that the food and air requirements of the Artonuee are measureably less than those of the Delanians. Thus we are able to load more Artonuee per ship. While we have always labored to the utmost to be fair and more than fair, we will not consider cutting the size of the juplee and iffling reserves." She sat. The members of the conference were silent.

"May we proceed with other business?" she asked, smiling. "The first item on the agenda deals with the readiness of the star fleet, I believe."

Argun, President of the Delanians, cleared his throat. "Lady," he said, and Miaree, looking at Rei, saw Rei's eyes shift quickly to Argun. "Our scientists, too, have studied the matter of Artonuee reproduction. It is their conclusion that the continuation of the Artonuee race can be assured with half the number of ifflings, and thus, half the number of ships devoted to the growing of juplee trees."

"Argun," she said. "I have made clear our feeling. It is unthinkable to an Artonuee not to have an iffling waiting. The ratio has already been reduced from surplus to one iffling for each Artonuee. Our people would not agree to such a course of action. There are deep religious convictions—"

"Damn religion," Argun said, his deep voice harsh. "We're talking about the lives of living Delanians, not bugs crawling around eating tree leaves."

In the shocked silence, Miaree looked wide-eyed at Rei. There was a pained expression on his face.

"Let's remember this," Argun said. "Since there are 6 billion of us and only 1.5 billion of you, we have agreed that all Artonuee go. Do you know what this means? It means, short of a miracle which I don't think is going to happen, that over a billion more of our people will have to be left behind. Over a billion people, sizzling on worlds which are not even their own. Do you like that picture?"

He was addressing Miaree. "No, Argun," she said. "It is a terrible picture."

"It is a picture which I do not intend to see," Argun said, his voice low.

"We will continue to build to the end," Rei said. "There is hope."

"Build with what?" Argun demanded. "Dirt and straw?" He rose. "Our miners are working in heat which kills. We've burrowed so deeply into five planets that we're near the heated magma. We've lost ten thousand men on that damned sun planet. And we're not producing enough metal per six months to build one star ship."

"We're putting more ships on the Seberian run," Miaree said.

The others were quiet, faces moving to follow the three way dialog.

"The Artonuee female lays six or more eggs," Argun said. "On a fertile planet the transplanted juplee trees carried by the fleet are capable of doubling themselves in fifteen years. By cutting the juplee fleet in half we do not threaten the race. When we find new planets, the iffling population can be replenished within two years."

"It is a matter of age-old belief," Miaree said, looking toward Rei for help.

"Beliefs change," Argun said harshly. "I have issued orders to convert fifty juplee ships to carry people. *People.* Living, intelligent beings."

"You have ordered," Miaree gasped, standing to face the tall Delanian. "How dare you?"

"I dare because there is necessity," Argun said. "I dare because I have seen enough of my people die."

"Your orders will be rescinded," Miaree said, her eyes purple with anger.

"Other instructions went out with that order," Argun said. "Delanians, stand."

Around the table the aliens rose, Rei among them. And as they stood, the eyes of the Artonuee present were drawn to evil-looking hand weapons, revealed when the Delanians opened their ceremonial cloaks.

"You have diverted resources to the making of weapons?" Miaree asked, unbelieving.

"They came with us," Argun said. "They occupied little space, added little weight. Not one Delanian was left behind because of the weapons. And because of the weapons, not one Delanian will be left behind when the fleet abandons the Artonuee system."

"Rei," Miaree whispered, looking at him. He could not meet her eye. "Oh, Rei."

23

Five was a world in the grip of organized chaos. With all but official roller vehicles long since consigned to the smelters to reclaim their metals, the artificially heated landscape flowered with the brilliance of Artonuee females moving toward central points. For some, there had been tearful farewells. For others, fortune had not even allowed that much. With them now were the stolid males of the race, grey, serious, silent. Already the shuttles were lifting, burning the atmosphere and gliding out of sight toward dark space, where the star fleet orbited. From the loading points, ranks of the huge ships were grouped in squadrons, closely packed. The laden ships hummed with life. There, inside the metal wombs which would carry the race through endles space, the sorrow of leave-taking was eased somewhat by the excitement of discovery, by carefully trained wardens who ordered and begged and yelled and coaxed the incomers into their proper compartments.

Dress rehearsal for the great adventure.

There in space, where the Fires of God gleamed in deadly nearness, the Artonuee tasted destiny.

Below, a heavy, aged male crouched over a workbench, ignoring the sounds from the outside world. Bertt had been notified. Already his section of the planet had been evacuated of Artonuee. In the dwelling around him Delanians prowled, seeking useful objects discarded by the departing Artonuee. A mile away, a section of the dwelling area burned, and there were none to halt the spread of the flames. Indeed, there was little need, for the fires were small in relation to the flames of doom which flickered in the sky, strong enough now to be visible, dwarfing the distant sun.

Bertt worked on.

"I am Bertt, once Overlord of the Fleet," he had told them when they stood, armed, on his portal and demanded that he join the others in the long line toward the shuttle pads.

"You are Artonuee, and you will leave with the others," he was told.

But rank had its privileges. A quick call to planet headquarters, and he was left in peace. Even the Delanians remembered that it was Bertt who had wedded the convertors to the fusion engine, making possible the giant ships which sparkled in near space, visible to the naked eye now that loading was underway.

Once before he had been given a deadline. Then he had failed.

There was the possibility of failure now, he admitted, as his shaking fingers made the last cold connection. What he planned was risky. The work of a lifetime depended on the function of a tiny loop added to the altered mires expander before him. That insignificant looking bit, encased in cold plastics, would have strained Bertt's ability to communicate, had he been asked to explain. It was the result of months of work, years of thought, and its simplicity, when added to Bertt's theory, wrought a tremendous change in the actions of the circuits. Basically, the loop fed electrons back onto themselves in a uni-field, a closed area which was physically no bigger than the ball of Bertt's spatulate fourth finger, but which had shown infinite capacity in his tests.

Bertt, himself, did not understand. But it was not necessary to understand. It was necessary only to make the final test.

Finished, he called, absently left his communicator on as he waited. There would be no one there, once he had gone, to use the instrument.

There was more difficulty as he joined the Artonuee packed into orderly lines at the shuttle pads, but once again, although he felt guilty to pass up the staring eyes of his fellows, rank allowed privilege, and he was escorted by two armed Delanian men to the work shuttle, allowed to carry his small case containing a few tools and the expander.

He breathed a sigh of relief when he saw that his personal powered flyer was still in its dock. Then he was inside, moving under control direction past the shuttles, the waiting star ships with air locks connected to other shuttles which disgorged Artonuee into the five-mile-long hulls.

His flight plan had listed Nirrar as his destination, but once free of Fivegate control, he executed a smooth turn and pointed the rounded nose of his flyer toward deep space. Once there, he allowed the flyer to drift powerless as he made the substitution, his altered expander replacing the mires expander in the flyer's power system.

Once his fingers would have flown over the work and the change would have been done in minutes. Now his hands shook with age and the task was irksome. When it was completed, he rested, his eyes closed, his heart laboring. When his pulse had slowed, he refreshed himself, then punched test circuits into play and watched with squinted lids, the results. They were satisfactory. He breathed deeply, ran the convertor to full power, the fusion engine giving headway toward deep space. His course had been planned years previously, a course which punched a straight-line hole through space for a distance of ten parsecs. The line ended outside the bounds of the galaxy, near a small, isolated cluster. The distance was incredibly far, roughly equivalent to the distance which separated the Artonuee system from the dead worlds of the Delanians, worlds now consumed in a huge ball of stellar fire which filled that sector of the galaxy. It was a distance which would take a light twenty ship over a year and a half to travel.

Bertt covered the distance in the time it took him to exhale after activating the drive. He rode, inertialess, on the force of the electrons in two 0.1-inch cubes of red metal. Against such force even God's Constant was insignificant. With the activation of the altered mires expander, changed beyond dreams by Bertt's theory and a small, plastic-enclosed loop which became a hole in space, Bertt the builder unleashed a new force into the universe and rode it like a thought down a line ten parsecs long, and then, waiting for something to happen, not realizing that it had, he looked out to see a sky unlike any he'd ever known. Ahead and to his left was the cluster, huge now, individual stars distinct, the nearer ones disced. Behind him was his galaxy. With the viewer on magnification, he could see the collisions as the two galaxies edged into each other, the point of star impact a mass of fire.

The man who had made infinite star travel possible, the male who, upon his return, would relieve two races of the necessity of decades, perhaps centuries of travel in the star ships, that male, Bertt, feeling joy in his heart, knelt before his flyer's controls and made a prayer to God.

His prayer of thanks still in his mind, he returned in a wink to the original position just outside the orbit of gutted Five, performed the journey again and again, leaping parsecs instantly, not even feeling the vast power which defied every known physical law. Emboldened by the ease of it, he calculated an extended course and in the same wink of time blasted past the distant globular cluster into intergalactic space, there to see, for the first time, the wheels of the colliding galaxies small in the viewer's magnification.

From afar, they were an object of mere astronomical beauty, cold, distant. It was difficult to think that twenty-four billion minds had perished there on the Delanian worlds, almost impossible to leave the triumph of deep space for the sorrow and turmoil of the home worlds. In a wink, he could be there, in a far galaxy. He could leave it all behind and be the first Artonuee to explore the vast deeps of the universe.

But he was Bertt, builder, and he had built the ultimate vehicle, and he would share his joy with them, his people, and with his friends, the Artonuee.

The fusion-powered journey from the orbit of Five to New World and then down to Government Quad at Nirrar consumed enough time for Bertt to circumnavigate the known universe.

24

Miaree lived a nightmare. For the first time in the history of the Artonuee, the dwelling of the Mother was under armed guard. And the guards were powerful, uniformed Delanians. Although, on the surface, nothing had changed, she felt undercurrents of threat, felt fur-tingling moments of dread.

"Lady," Rei had assured her, "it is for your own protection. Many of our people have seen the Fires. Many left the home worlds just ahead of destruction. They had to bid farewell to friends and sons, knowing that they would never see them again. Now they are told that the tragedy must be repeated. True, it will be on a smaller scale, but those who have experienced the terror, who were lucky enough to be given space on a ship once, fear with knowledge that they might be selected out this second time."

"Does this, then, justify the wanton slaughter of Artonuee on Outworld?" Miaree asked, shaking her head tiredly.

"An isolated incident. We moved the Army in as soon as reports of the violence reached us."

"The Army," she said. "There is not even such a word in our language."

Rei turned from her, paced to a viewer, looked down moodily onto the Quad below.

"The evacuation from Five continues to be orderly and effective," he said at last.

"So it begins," she said. She was thinking of the females of Five, torn from the arms of the lovers who had become their lives. And a future of infinite sadness loomed before her.

"There is much to consider," Rei said. "The Light Twenty Scouts in the second arm have made astronomical findings which are encouraging. Their scannings have located no less than five stars whose orbital movements indicate the presence of planets."

She would grow old without him. She would seek her iffling in the confines of a metal ship and not under the warm sun of the Artonuee. Never again would she walk the Great Bloom. Five hatchings, and she had yet to look on the beauty of a living egg.

On Outworld, the planet of art and beauty, Delanian women had first torn the wings from and then killed a female caught in a love merge with a Delanian man. And the violence had spread to terrorize an entire dwelling area. Now the star ships were converging on Outworld to move those who loved it most forever, first to The World, then—

"Old Bertt has been asking for an audience," Rei said. "Have you yet seen him?"

"I have not been informed." So, at last, he was homecoming. She did not want to see him, did not want to have to face that last bit of sadness. Yet, she had invited. "Will you have him called?"

He was aged and stooped. When she saw him last, he showed his maturity, and she had not suspected that homecoming was so near for him; but with a male, especially, the end, once upon him, approached with astounding suddenness. "Dear Bertt," she said, rising, touching his shaking arm. "We will provide you with transportation. The fleet lies, half loaded, off The World. The ifflings crunch happily in the lighted holds. There you will seed the life which will fly with us."

"I have waited for five days, Lady," Bertt said.

"Here?" She was puzzled.

"First the Delanian guards. Then, when I was

passed, the Delanians below, in the lower levels. Has the Mother, then, been relegated to a small office in an upper floor, there to consort with her man," he spat the word, "and forget the greatness of our race?"

"Discourtesy does not become you," she said, saddened. "I accept your censure, however, as mine. The duties of the office . . ." She paused, for there was a vacant look on Bertt's face. Was there so little time for him?

"I could have stayed," he said, his lips scarcely moving. "I could have traveled like the wings of thought to see the heart of the universe, to search out the nooks and hiding places of creation itself."

God, she thought, he is already rambling. Then, as she reached out to him, he straightened, became for a moment the Bertt of old. Pride gleamed in his eyes. "Let it be recorded," he said, "that an Artonuee male made it. That Bertt, the builder, did it."

"Bertt?"

"You once gave me a month, Lady, to change the known universe. It took longer, I fear." He chuckled. "But I, Bertt, have flown—no, not flown, for it is more than that. I have been moved by a power which dwarfs the fusion engines of the Delanians. I have traveled a hundred parsecs in the wink of an eye, My Lady."

There was a feeling about him. She shared it, felt his triumph, believed him. "Bertt," she whispered. "It works?"

He nodded, his shoulders slumping. "May I sit, Lady?"

"Of course," she said, taking his arm to lead him to a chair.

To share the news, she called a hasty conference. When it was convened, there were only her Artonuee officials and advisors present.

"The Delanians sent word that they had more important things," said Lady Caee.

"Rei, too?" Miaree asked.

"He, at least, was more polite," Caee answered. "He

begged to be excused for an hour, until the council of the Delanian chiefs is ended."

"Perhaps," Miaree said, with a shiver of dread, "it is best that we first share the joy of Bertt, the builder, among ourselves."

Bertt stood proudly. His words brought a hush over the gathered Artonuee.

When he had finished, it was the priest, Ceelen, who spoke. "God has indeed forgiven us."

"Where was God," asked Lady Belle, "when the Delanian women pulled the wings from dozens of our females?" Belle had changed. Her eyes brooded purple, her face showed the harsh lines of tension. "Lady Mother, I respectfully suggest that we consider keeping this an Artonuee secret." There was a gasp around the table. "Over two hundred Artonuee died on Outworld, Lady. More will die. I feel it. There is talk in the streets that it will be Artonuee who face the Fires, not Delanians, as we now believe."

"That is nonsense," Miaree said.

"Is it nonsense, Lady," asked Bertt, "to see the Government Quad swarm with armed Delanians, to see Artonuee excluded from their own seat of government?"

"Already, they have struck at the heart of our life, at our most basic beliefs," said Diere, Overlady of Research. "The order to cut the juplee-carrying ships by half their number was issued without consultation with us."

"Millions of sacred ifflings will perish," said Caee. "If the Delanians are capable of that, of what else are they capable?"

"We have worked together, my children," the priest Ceelen said, "but at what cost?"

"It is possible, Lady," Bertt said. "The fleets will be segregated. We will be alone. The necessary hardware can be produced in the ships' shops, and the installation can be made while in flight. Then, at the appointed time, the Delanians will merely see nothing. The Artonuee fleet will disappear into deep space in the wink of a lash, and there, with unlimited mobility, we can seek new worlds. The universe will be open to us. No longer will we be faced with the Fires of God, for we can leave these doomed galaxies. We can seek over numberless parsecs, and in the vast universe find homes which will see the continuation of Artonuee life for an eternity."

"And leave the Delanians to roam empty space at light-times-twenty for, perhaps, centuries?" She shook her head. "Have you no shame, any of you?"

"I have merely to look at our worlds," Caee said. "I have merely to remember how a young female, wings plucked from her, wept not for her pain but for the loss of her man. Those of us who are free of the Delanians"—she cast a meaningful glance toward Miaree—"know that our relationship with them was a terrible drug which distracted us from our purpose in life. It is said, among some of our people, that the universal attempt to bed our Artonuee females was indeed a plot to love us out of existence. I, for one, do not know whether there was a plot, but there might as well have been: Delanian-induced sterility in our females was a fact. No female, on her own, had the will power to sunder herself from her lover long enough to produce fertile eggs. In a generation, had not the threat of the Fires forced the Delanians to take more direct action, we would have been extinct."

"Nonsense," Miaree said heatedly. "Don't you see, all of you, that dear Bertt's invention has solved all our problems? We have been allowed a bit more time, thanks to God. It is enough. If the conversion is so simple, then it can be accomplished in months. The first ships can be operating on Bertt's principle within weeks. At speeds which shrink the galaxy to insignificance, our ships can explore millions of stars. And before it is too late, before a single Delanian or a single Artonuee dies in the Fire, we can have located habitable planets. At Bertt's speeds, we can make many trips to and from those planets. We can move everyone.

25

Rei himself almost came to think of it as God's will. Soon, he chuckled, as he watched the production lines pour out the altered circuits and hardware for the Bertt Engine, I'll be praying to the God of the Artonuee. For he had flown in Bertt's own ship, had seen the universe dwindle, had felt an exultation which filled him even now, as he pursued his new task of seeing to the installation of the new expanders on all of the fleet.

But, if the God of the Artonuee was great, that made old Bertt greater, didn't it? Bertt had beat God at Her own game.

There was a light in Miaree's eyes. She bloomed. The cares of the past years seemed to fall from her, leaving her as he had known her first, there on Outworld. Nor was he the only one to see the light of love and joy in Artonuee eyes. Quietly, privately, Delanian officials, who had obeyed their own edict to leave off their delightful activities with the daughters of the Artonuee, were reclaiming their mistresses. Argun, bellowing with pleasure, had immediately summoned his favorite.

The news had been spread. The sense of fear and doom which had hung over the five worlds was lessened to an almost carnival atmosphere. The evacuation of Artonuee from Outworld and New World, under way, was proceeding in a spirit of good will and the lines of boarding Artonuee could be heard to sing.

167

No one was happier than Rei. A terrible burden had been lifted from him. No longer would he be forced to hide his true feelings from Miaree. In short weeks, they would embark together on the greatest of all adventures. Together, they would explore the universe.

At the end of a rewarding day, he made his way to her rooms and there, in a glow of love, idled away the evening, resenting it with all his heart when the communication room allowed a call from Argun to be put through. He was a Delanian, and when he was called by his President, he went.

He found Argun with his female, nude, sated. The female was dismissed, and she smiled back at them as she stepped lightly from the room. Argun shrugged into a robe and drank. "Damn," he said, "I'm glad I found that one. She's a freak. Two sets of those incredible muscles." He laughed with gusto. "She's pleased as hell that she's going on the ship with me."

"Oh?" Rei asked. "I've seen no indication that the segregation order has been rescinded."

"Damn, man, you've had it good. While the rest of us were going without Artonuee cunt for the sake of appearances, you were warming the bed of one of the best-looking bugs I've seen."

Rei hid his displeasure.

"Sure," Argun said. "I'm taking her. She's young. Just off The World. Just finished her education. She'll last me the rest of my life before she fades."

"Will others be granted this same privilege?" Rei asked. For the question of his being with Miaree on the flight was still unresolved. As Mother of all the Artonuee she could order him to be with her, but he knew she would not do so unless the same was allowed for all her sisters.

"We'll have room for almost a million of them," Argun said. "Mostly female, although some of the higher placed women might want to take along a little male pet."

Rei felt his neck tingle. He felt cold. "That's changed, sir. That's all changed."

Argun roared. "Damn, boy, I told you long ago that you're too soft. You've let this female-dominated society get to you." He looked directly into Rei's eye. "Nothing has changed. From the time you submitted your first report to me, outlining your plan to fuck the Artonuee out of existence by loving hell out of all the females, it hasn't changed. Damn, man, our women won't stand still for this type of crap forever. We've got the universe open to us. You want to throw away the chance to populate it with Delanians because of a sweet little bug with an active cunt?"

26

"Lady," said Diere, Overlady of Research, "it is a curious thing, this. I have been checking the reports of the Light Twenty Scout ships which have for years past been searching the near stars for habitable planets. I discover that all of the scouts now on station are manned by our people, by Artonuee males. And it has struck me that times have changed. In years past, we females were the daring ones, the flyers. Males plodded on the earth and, at best, worked the mining drivers and operated the slow, ponderous shuttle craft."

"It is for the best," Miaree said wearily. "We have learned well from the Delanians. Now male and female work side by side in our society as in theirs." Then she paused, mused. "All scouts on station are flown by Artonuee?"

"Here is the list," Diere said.

She took the duppaper copies and ran her eyes down. The most distant scouts were years of travel time from the home worlds. All of the small ships were flown by Artonuee. A terrible thought came to her, a thought which she would not, could not accept. Instead, she tossed her head and smiled. "We must send orders for all of them to return. Their slow progress through the stars is no longer necessary. See to it, Diere." On second thought. "Make a memo to Rei to suggest that during their scouting runs the new Bertt ships rendezvous with the most distant scouts and pick them up."

"It will be done," Diere said.

The evacuation of Outworld was complete. A full half of the total number of Artonuee were back home. The shuttles were at work all over New World, lifting the remaining Artonuee to the waiting star ships for the short trip to the home planet. In Government Quad, thousands of clerks were transferring the records of the Artonuee to microtape so that history would ride with the race on the journey into the distant stars. The seat of Artonuee government would soon be abandoned, the Mother herself taking her place with her people on The World.

Rei was absent, with the fleet at Five. Although she missed him with all her heart, she was proud that her man was taking such a vital part in this moment of history. Rei would plan and dispatch the Bertt ships to move instantly through the galaxy. Miaree was confident that within a short time the good news would come winging back, the news of the discovery of a suitable number of good planets. Then, with time to spare, the movement of peoples would begin, the huge ships making trip after trip, shifting populations and their goods. Nothing need be left behind.

She busied herself checking the lists being prepared by her staff, lists of government files and machinery which would be salvaged once the point of destination had been determined. She would move only those records necessary for immediate administration to The World for the brief stay there. Later, the entire bulk of government would be moved, intact, to a new home on a new world.

It was a time-consuming task. Meanwhile, she was kept abreast of evacuation on the planet and was pleased to see that it went smoothly. The efficient Delanians had learned well from the evacuation of Five and Outworld, and a planet was emptied of its original inhabitants within weeks of the beginning of the movement. She herself waited only for the return of Rei, to hear his personal report of the departure of the first Bertt ships to seek new worlds.

From her high rooms, she could look down onto the spaces of the Quad. There was an eerie feeling of strangeness about it, for there were only Delanians there. Another Artonuee world had been given over, if only temporarily, to the aliens.

Once, while resting, she saw a lone female, wings exposed in the style of the Delanian-mated, being escorted by a tall man. She knew that some alliances had been renewed when the news of Bertt's miraculous breakthrough was announced, but she noted that where the pair walked, the heads of Delanian women followed them. She shuddered involuntarily, thinking of the violent treatment of Artonuee females on Outworld.

She was isolated in her tower. She had communication with the administration offices on The World, but feeling rather guilty for not being there, she left the settlement of her people on their home world to assistants. She was, she knew, being frightfully self indulgent by staying on New World, but she rationalized her failure to be with her people by telling herself that it was important that the first lady know all details of the explorations. This time of trial and sadness would pass, and on new worlds the Artonuee, the universe opened to them, would rise to a greatness never before dreamed.

It was old Bertt who brought the terrible news. He had been supervising the installation of the last new expanders. He flew into Nirrar in his own vehicle, forced his way through the armed guards at no little cost to his temper and his dignity, and faced her, his male eyes reddened with madness.

"Lady," he said, his voice strange, "star ships are being loaded on both Five and Outworld."

"The explorers," Miaree said.

"Population," Bertt said. "Delanians."

Her hand at her throat, she felt weakness. "There must be a reason," she said.

"Even now the final off-loading of Artonuee is being completed on The World," Bertt said. "Do you have explanation for this, Lady?"

Miaree, fighting the dread, punched the communicator. "Please get me Fleet Overlord Rei, on the planet Five," she ordered, her voice firm in spite of her fears.

"Sorry, baby," a male Delanian voice said. "They've taken away all your toys."

"I beg your pardon?" Miaree said. "Where is Tanle, my communications officer? I want to speak with her."

"There is no one here," the voice said. The communicator fell silent.

Eyes darkened with fear and rage, she ran to the door, into the hallway. Diere's office was empty. The personal art objects always clearly visible on Diere's desk were missing. As she ran out of the empty office, she almost screamed with delight, for Rei was coming out of the lift, tall, handsome. Rei would explain. Rei would reprimand the Delanians below who had been discourteous. Rei would assure her that Bertt's information was not what it seemed. She ran to him, threw herself into his arms. He held her close, and then looked down into her disturbed eyes.

Bertt stood in the doorway of Miaree's office. Looking over Miaree's head, Rei saw the grimness of the old male's face. "You know, then," he said softly to Miaree.

The Fires of God would have been more merciful. They, at least, would have been quick and final. In the Fires, she would not have become a walking dead female.

"Why?" she asked simply, not weeping.

"It was not my decision," he said. "You must believe that."

"Please," she said. "I want to be with my people, if you don't mind."

"No," he said gently.

She looked into his eyes.

"You may take anything you like, things of a personal nature," Rei said. "We will be together."

"And my people?" she asked.

"You told me once, Miaree, of the extermination of the animals of The World."

"We are not animals," she said calmly.

"No, of course you are not. But there was a choice. It was a terrible choice. The decision of our leaders was dictated by the death of twenty-four billion Delanians."

"But there is time. The new ships—"

"I asked them to give you just one ship," he said. "I begged them. I begged for just one ship to allow the race to live."

"We can find planets. We can shuttle people. There is time."

He shook his head sadly. "Our people are filled with fear. The Fires can be seen, as they were seen on the home worlds. We began the loading on Five to prevent the outbreak of a popular uprising."

"In the name of God," she said, "there is room in the universe for all."

"Once we had gods. There was a god for every purpose. The gods lived up there, in the Fires. When we were a young race and saw the Fires moving gradually, slowly, crawling toward us, our cultists rejoiced and said that the gods were favoring us, moving their dwelling to be nearer our planet. When we went into space on primitive rockets, it was to search for the gods, and we found only cold death and terrible vacuum. By then we understood that there were no gods living in the Fires unless they ate ionized electrons and thrived on hard radiation and swam on the seas of a burning star. There is no God, Miaree, only radiation and cold and fire and death and the accident of life, which is precious only to those who are strong enough to fight for it. We have fought and we have lost. We have paid a terrible price in dead, and we have learned that the universe is basically inhospitable to life and only the strongest will survive.

"The decision to abandon the Artonuee was not coldly selfish. There is real doubt that your race would survive transplanting. Your life chain is fragile, depending on an exact set of conditions, soil, air, sun, which may not be matchable anywhere in the universe. The percentage of rare earths in the soil of The World is a unique situation. Have you never wondered why the juplee forests were confined to The World, why it was necessary to lavish constant care on the trees which were taken, for example, to Outworld, for decorative and spiritual purposes? No. It was decided, by those in command, that moving the Artonuee was a gamble. And we would have been gambling with over a billion more Delanian lives. It is regrettable and tragic, but there is no escape from the basic fact that we Delanians are more suited for the rigors of space and planet change."

She had ceased to listen. She had pulled away, looking at him in horror. Behind her, Bertt was weeping silently. She turned to him, took his arm.

"I will come for you," Rei said. "And for the worthy Bertt, who will rest here with you until it is time."

She escorted the old male to her chambers, seated him comfortably. His eyes were wet with his weeping. "It was I," he said. "I made it possible. First I gave them the union of convertor and fusion, then I gave them the power of unopposed electrons. It was I who gave, My Lady."

"Yes, yes, you meant well, Bertt. You are not to be blamed."

He dried his eyes, his cheeks. A strength seemed to flow into his old body. There was a look of pride and decision on his face. "I gave," he said, "but I saw the contempt on their faces. Once, while I was Overlord of the Fleet, I heard workers talking. 'All of the bugs,' they said; they called us bugs, a Delanian word full of derision. 'All of the bugs are going,' they said. And I recognized then the basis of our relationship, but I would not admit it. I worked with Untell. I shared my bed with Untell and it was good. And I would not open my eyes to see that they were using us, that they were taking the last resources of our worlds, using our worlds as a base for a further leap away from the Fires. There were jokes, even then, about loving the Artonuee out of existence. But I told myself that a great race, a race which could reach the stars, could not commit such a vast conspiracy."

"Have you thought, dear Bertt, that our priests have been proven right?" She was numb. Her heart beat, but she was dead. "Nothing has changed, really. Before they came we were to face the Fires. Now we still face the Fires. It is even ironically fitting that we face them on the old world, the home planet."

Bertt seemed not to hear. He sat straight, eyes hard, glittering. "I would not believe until, finished with the installation of my gift on all the star ships, I saw with my own eyes the loading of Delanians on Five. And then I praised that male jealousy which had forced me to do it."

"What did you do?"

"Do you think we males have enjoyed seeing you, our Mother, seeing our females going to the Delanian men with such joy? Oh, we took the lesser prize, the Delanian women, and we told ourselves that we were enjoying the best of two worlds, for the women were ever ready for pleasure and the eternal stink of pleele, the stifling smell of our females' constant readiness—yes, I say stink. Once it was a pleasure, but in massive amounts as it radiated out from all females, it became a stink in our nostrils and it insured our own constant readiness, which we burned on the bodies of the fleshy women. And we knew in our hearts that the pleasures of flesh were not God's will, not the destiny of the Artonuee, and we grieved privately. And I thought of this as I designed the fleet. Thank God, I thought of it."

"I don't understand," Miaree said.

"You will, my daughter. They need me, for I alone know the secrets of the altered expanders. So I will be carried along, a prize, a slave, a worker to teach their technicians the secrets of my inventions. You will go—"

"No," she said.

"Yes, you must. I am too old. I might fail, there in the depths of space. I might seek my iffling and find no iffling to accept the life force which cries out to be exchanged. And then you will have to complete the job."

"What job?" She stood before him. "Are these just the ramblings of an old male? Explain to me, Bertt. Tell me."

"When the time is right," Bertt said, and would speak no more.

27

Poised in deep space off the orbit of Five, the fleet stretched into the distance, its numbers, rank on rank, assembled in order, under the direct control of the flagship on the center point. Behind it, four worlds were empty. A fifth, The World, swarmed with the total population of the Artonuee. There, hunger stalked, for a gutted world, its surface scarred by strip mining, its resources melted now into the metal hides of the fleet, could not support the race. The mutilated juplee forests were but a fraction of their former glory. Artonuee died and their loves were dead with them, their life force wasted, fading into empty air in the absence of ifflings; for in the end, the loaded iffling ships had belched their sacred cargo out into a spiral orbit leading to eventual disintegration in the sun. A forest of juplee, emptied into cold space, made but a minor ripple on the surface of the Artonuee star. Ifflings, long dead in the vacuum, were mere motes as they were drawn into the furnace.

Her cubicle was small. She was allowed freedom, but she was among aliens who looked at her and resented her presence. There were others of her kind, the mistresses of the high officials, but when she passed them she lowered her eyes, shamed to be one of them. Bertt was there, treated with a certain condescending honor. Once she heard Argun speak to the old male.

"Good work," the tall Delanian said, when Bertt had

finished an adjustment to the expander. "I'm glad you're here to see it."

Then, when Bertt, older and weaker, had shambled away, Argun laughed. "Of course, we'd have discovered it sooner or later, eh? And after all, he probably laid the foundation for it when he was working with our Untell."

Bertt seemed to accept the situation. He was interested in nothing but his work. A short jump was scheduled to test the central control system; the fleet had never operated as a unit, and in order to maintain contact in the spaces between galaxies—it having been announced that the plan was to leave the stricken galaxies far behind and seek entire new universes—the expanders of all ships were now linked to central control. The short test jump was calculated to end within distances which could be covered by communication, thus allowing any ship left behind by a malfunctioning expander to rejoin the fleet.

There was perfection. With the touch of a button, Bertt sent a fleet numbering in six figures, possessing a mass equal to that of a small planet, leaping the specified distance to come out of the jump in perfect formation, not one ship out of line.

On a course plotted to close on a distant galaxy across parsecs of space, the fleet leaped again, taking the distance in fractions of the total journey, lest miscalculation send the fleet, like a colliding galaxy, into the midst of dense stars. It was then, at the end of the first huge jump, that a minor malfunction disrupted instruments at the control center on the flagship. There was a worried look on the cold face of Argun as Bertt ran tests with his slow, shaking fingers. After a series of adjustments, Bertt stood erect.

"I will need the aid of an Artonuee," he said.

"We have techs who can help you," Argun said.

"The female, Miaree," Bertt insisted. "It is a delicate adjustment needing the abilities of the Artonuee eye. Bring her."

She was summoned from her cubicle. She had not seen Rei since the loading, but he was there, standing beside Bertt in front of the exposed wiring of the console. She averted her eyes.

Bertt spoke to her in the language of the Artonuee, a mixture of thought and sound undetectable to the alien ears. He chose his words carefully, not using sounds which could have given any clue to his meaning. His words were old, old language, bringing with them a glow of pride. Even in defeat, Miaree saw, the Artonuee were great.

"It is time, Mother Miaree."

At first she thought that he was speaking personally, for his face was gaunt and strained. His physical movements were slow and tortured. For weeks he had seemed to live on will alone, long past his appointed time, far from the ravaged world of the ifflings.

But, no. Speaking now in Delanian, he said, "I require a measure of the field of the fleet. My flyer is based in Scout Bay Five. Board it. Remove yourself to a distance of—"

"Hold it," Argun said. "That can be done by a man."

"Can the eyes of a man see a magnetic field?" Bertt asked. He turned his back on the tall man. "When you are at the assigned point, we will communicate."

She looked toward Argun for confirmation. Her heart pounded. Although Bertt had not explained his reasons, she sensed that the time, the time he had promised, was near.

"We must hurry," he said. "Hurry, my daughter. I fail."

"Speak Delanian, damn you," Argun said.

Ignoring him, Bertt caught himself, lest he fall in weakness. "You will teach them, my Mother Miaree. You will return home."

"Stop that damned squeaking," Argun said angrily.

Miaree bowed respectfully toward the leader. "He is old, Lord. His mind rambles."

"Then move, bitch, before he dies on us," Argun ordered.

As she turned, her eyes flashed across his face. There was a coldness there. The coldness was ice in her heart.

The flyer to be used for scouting was an old Bertt, Class VI, improved. Conversion had been so rapid that time had not allowed for removal of its sails. After it was expelled from the lock of the star ship it handled beautifully.

She had not been in a flyer, alone in space, for many years. Space was dark and warmer than the hearts of the Delanians. It was familiar. It was loved. With deft fingers she burned the fusion engine, took her position. She saw the fleet through the viewer, individual ships magnified to the size of her fingertips. The units of the fleet covered volumes of space, each squadron separated by a distance which once would have taken days to travel. She activated her communication system.

"I am in position," she said.

It was Rei's voice. "The old man is ill."

"God," breathed Miaree silently.

"Wait," Rei said. "I will hold the communicator to his mouth."

"Tell them," she heard in Artonuee. "Tell them." There were shuffling sounds, Bertt's voice, weak, quavering, speaking Delanian now, "Hold me to the console."

"He is standing," Rei said.

"Expanding," Bertt mumbled. "Read, daughter."

With tears in her eyes, knowing his terrible pain, she read the field of the fleet, her eyes opening to see. She reported.

"Jump ... one-tenth unit ..." He was speaking Artonuee.

She heard Argun's harsh voice. "Now wait a minute," he said.

She jumped. She turned the flyer. The fleet was now distant, tiny in the viewer.

"Time," she heard the weak, tired voice say. "Tell—"

"He has fainted," Rei said. "What else did he want, Miaree?"

"I don't know," she said. Was it, then, to end like this?

"He speaks," Rei said. "Wait."

"I cannot ..." Bertt said, his voice weak. "I fail, Mother."

"You cannot fail," she said, her voice musical, sweet, in the native language. "Bertt, hear me. There is one thing to do. You alone know. Speak. Move, Bertt. Stand for one last time."

"I cannot, Lady. But the power is also yours. On the expander controls you will see ... a switch."

"Bertt ..."

Silence.

"He is dead, Miaree."

"God rest," she said.

She was an old flyer hand. She had noted the switch. And the tiny symbol engraved on it, the ancient, religious symbol denoting God's Fires. Hidden under an overhanging bank of controls, it would have defied a casual glance from any but Artonuee. And she had guessed.

She, too, had the power.

Before her, the fleet stretched, its squadrons ordered. Six billion beings breathed and felt fears and knew hopes and enjoyed the love which was now denied her.

"Miaree, you may return. He is dead."

Rei's voice.

Rei's living voice, living after him.

The lag of long seconds as his voice came at light speed brought his last words to her just ahead of the birth of a thousand new stars in the velvet blackness of intergalactic space. Rei himself was gone before his words came to her, was nothing more than scattered particles before the fires blossomed.

The old male, knowing well the forces trapped

within his cold plastic holes which led into a space not known to the universe, knowing the destructive forces of unopposed electrons in the millions of cubes of soft metal which were a vital part of all the fleet's expanders, knowing all this, and knowing, too, his long, logical hatred, the old male had planned well. Unchanneled, the incredible forces of unopposed electrons had, with the touch of her finger on a tiny switch, returned sanity to a universe gone mad.

The vast explosions had imparted motion before total disintegration. The vectors were random, scattering the electrons of the fleet in a flaring pattern which moved away from the home galaxies in the direction of the expansion of the universe.

The released energies rushed out toward her distant flyer at sub-light speeds, giving her moments to watch in awe as the final construction of Bertt, the builder, avenged the Artonuee.

Yes, she would tell them. She would tell her people that they did not face doom in vain. She would tell them that their betrayal by those who had used love against them was avenged. She would say that the God of the Artonuee, although vengeful, was still God, allowing this one last gesture by Her doomed people. She would return to the ravaged planets and await, with her people, the Fires, knowing that the Delanians had howled themselves into oblivion before her.

Proud, straight in the control seat of the flyer, she watched the growing bloom of fire. She allowed herself only one moment of sadness. In that moment she saw his face, as he had looked that first night on Outworld.

Rei.

But nothing had changed. God had promised Fire. The coming of the Delanians had not changed, had only seemed to alter the inevitable. The Artonuee had seen the coming of an alien race, had loved with its members, had hoped; and there were still the Fires.

Miaree, proud Artonuee female, sat with exposed wings, with straight back.

God was God and was triumphant.

But there remained one final moment before she went home, there to muse, to repent, to communicate with that silent, all-powerful God.

In the early days, an ancient sister Artonuee had flown in space, using the wings of a sun, committing the original sin and exulting in it.

In the moments of the last days, a large-eyed, beautiful, prideful Artonuee female once again defied God. There were no tears as she watched the spread of the paroxysm which, in the wink of an eye, destroyed a race. There was a selfish, very Artonueeistic glow of exuberant joy as the debris of a fleet and of six billion Delanians and one old, tired, dead male Artonuee swept out toward the Bertt flyer, sails set, waiting to ride the whirlwind of the most titanic storm since the birth of the universe.

28

Alaxender has prepared some figures for us, my young friends. Perhaps they will be of interest even to those among you who, according to my informants, are having difficulty in electronic theory. Although I, being merely a literature teacher, have difficulty comprehending the theory of electricity—for the life of me I don't understand how something can move without anything moving—Alaxender sports the highest marks in his classes and he assures me that there is small chance of error in his figures.

The young man of Trojan has also written something regarding a new dimension, pertaining to what is called, in the text, Bertt's cold plastic hole in space; but such theories befuddle me even more than the proven ones, so we will confine ourselves to this. According to Alaxender, the soft metal used by Bertt could be nothing other than common copper. And much is known about that metal. For example, it is a fundamental law that an electron at rest, in copper, exerts a certain force on every other electron at rest, repelling its fellows in inverse proportion to the square of the distance between them. This force is measurable; it is 8.038×10^{-26} pounds.

When I first read young Alaxender's explanation of Bertt's Engine, I asked him, 'If there is such immense force there, why isn't every piece of copper blasted apart by it?' He assures me—and I am pleased to learn it, having an aversion to being penetrated by flying particles of copper—that there is a counter force, represented by a proton. A proton exactly balances an electron, very exactly indeed. If the repulsion of the protons were not exactly balanced against that of the electrons, then we could have a release of some rather impressive forces.

More figures, my young friends: We have read, in translation, the value of the force generated by the mutual repulsion of electrons in two one-tenth-of-an-inch cubes of copper placed one inch from each other. That force was six hundred billion tons. I hesitate to attempt the simple multiplication of the force if the cubes of copper had been, say, one inch to a side, much less six inches or a foot.

Alaxender assures me that, given the correctness of the translation, the force used by Bertt to drive his star ships and to destroy the Delanians could have been none other than that of the electrons in copper, somehow released by neutralizing the balancing force of the protons.

I am not qualified to comment on this. Others have commented, endlessly, before us. I understand that vast amounts of money have been spent in an effort to duplicate Bertt's discovery without success. I do not know enough about either subject to venture an opinion. (I refer not only to our research, but also to Alaxender's conclusion that it was electron force which pushed the star ships.) Frankly, I don't see any reason for us to seek such power, the blink drive being as efficient as it is, and hydrogen power being as easily produced as it is.

About LaConius' conclusion that the Q.S.S. phenomenon is explained by the legend, I make no statement beyond saying that perhaps the computer translators erred in the rendering of the title of this small volume. Could it be The Story of Miaree? Could it be The Life of Miaree? Or do we accept what literature classes have accepted for years and continue to call this book The Legend of Miaree?

If it is legend, why were the vast research projects instituted in an effort to discover Bertt's power?

Ah, but I express an opinion, after all.

There will be no class tomorrow. You may use this time to begin your final papers on the work we have just completed. Now, shall we break five minutes early? My favorite table in the dining hall has been usurped, of late, by a certain chemistry teacher. Today, perhaps, I can take possession before she arrives.

science fiction

from BALLANTINE

WALK TO THE END OF THE WORLD,
S. M. Charnas $1.25

ICERIGGER, Alan Dean Foster $1.25

UNDER PRESSURE, Frank Herbert $1.25

THE LEGEND OF MIAREE, Zach Hughes $1.25

THE BEST OF STANLEY G. WEINBAUM
With an INTRODUCTION by Isaac Asimov
and an Afterword by Robert Bloch $1.50

launching a new series of Sci Fi Greats

---

available at your local bookstore

To order by mail, send price of book(s) plus
25¢ per order for handling to Ballantine Cash
Sales, P.O. Box 505, Westminster, Maryland,
21157. Please allow three days for delivery.